# Catch & Release

*Also by Gus Willemin*

**Sideman**

*(Dancing Moon Press, 2014)*

Mike & Katie
Love ya both
Uncle Gus

# Catch & Release

a novel by

Gus Willemin

G Willemin
Newport, OR

DANCING MOON PRESS
NEWPORT, OREGON

*Catch & Release*



**Publisher's Note:** This book is a work of fiction. The characters, incidents, and dialogue are drawn from the author's imagination and are not to be construed as real. Any resemblance to actual events or persons, living or dead, is entirely coincidental.



Paperback ISBN: 978-1-937493-86-8
Ebook ISBN: 978-1-937493-87-5
Library of Congress Control Number: 2015912324

Willemin, Gus
Catch & Release
1. Fly-fishing—fiction; 2. Pacific Northwest—fiction; 3. Eagle Cap Wilderness—fiction; 4. Coming of Age—fiction; 5. Camping—fiction; 6. Family relationships—fiction; I. TITLE

Cover design & production: *Sarah Gayle, SolaLuna Studios*
Editing, book design & production: *Carla Perry, Dancing Moon Press*
Manufactured in the United States of America

DANCING MOON PRESS
P.O. Box 832, Newport, OR 97365; 541-574-7708
www.dancingmoonpress.com
info@dancingmoonpress.com

**FIRST EDITION**

*This book is dedicated to:*

Veronica and Amanda certainly,
Christopher in spirit,
and all those who encourage me to
keep on writing.

Thanks go to my editor, Carla Perry
of Dancing Moon Press,
and to Sarah Gayle of Sarah Gayle Art
for the cover art and design.

# Contents

# One: Twin

THE SECOND WEEK OF SEPTEMBER in Oregon is the best time of year—or so I have always thought. September is the month I am inevitably reminded of an earlier time in my life, a time shared as one of an identical pair. Born forty-two years ago as Kenneth Morrison, I lived my first twenty-one years as half of a set of twins with my brother, Kevin, and the following twenty-one years as an individual, solitary self. Now, in 2014, few in my circle of friends know anything about Kevin, but for this coming week, my former brothers-in-arms will be calling me "Twin."

For an entire week every September, I erase the past twenty years by reuniting with two other former Marines who, like me, live in Oregon. The three of us served together here in the States and in Iraq for one enlistment in our late teens.

I tiptoe my way through my house at 4 a.m. Maneuvering in the darkness, I try not to wake my wife and two stepdaughters as I quietly shower, reflecting that it would likely be a week before I could bathe again. I do a mental checklist of supplies I still need to pack before starting out on the first leg of my trip—the one-hour drive to Corvallis.

I'm proud of my organizational skills—mostly acquired since Kevin's departure. I've been prepared for this trip since long before the last of our summer vacationers departed, taking with them the remnants of traditional summer coastal fog. Just like Dorothy when she lands in Oz and the black and white of Kansas turns to Technicolor, so too does the Oregon Coast transform in autumn. Summers spent running a beachfront bed & breakfast leave me scant time for relaxation, or even thoughts about my own enjoyment. So, as in previous years, I've carved out a week for myself and look forward to the next seven days in nature.

From now until Halloween, my large home will be shared with retired couples and the occasional solitary traveler—easy enough work for my wife and two teenaged stepdaughters. Those three women were bred for the hospitality business, and have run this operation smoothly since long before I arrived.

Kathy was left as the sole owner of this bed and breakfast when her first husband decided the lifestyle was too much for him. She was courageously determined to stand fast and raise her two young children right here, and to her credit, she did a wonderful job for the many years before I came around. One daughter loves to cook for groups, and the other has been taught well by her mother to tend the edible food garden and grounds outside. That left me to assume the role of second husband, first stepfather, and back-up luggage carrier adept at fixing all dents to the place.

I don't wish to give the impression that Kathy, my first and only wife, makes her children do all the work. Quite the contrary. Along with her love of renovating old homes, Kathy has a discerning eye for décor. She arranges all living spaces so that they feel cozy and inviting, like a home away from home. Our house is clean, uncluttered and orderly, as well as comfortable, useful, and well loved. In a word, our bed and breakfast is *inviting,* an important aspect for travelers drawn to bed & breakfast lodging. Kathy has an eye for what appeals to vacationers, and she had all that in place long before I entered her life.

Much as I would like to take credit for this successful enterprise, the truth is it runs just fine without me, which always makes me realize how very fortunate I am. I have a family that can easily sustain itself during times when I go off to renew myself with seven days of camping adventures with my two good friends. I've done this annual trek for more than twenty years. Sometimes I think I've already experienced enough camping and fishing adventures to sustain any middle-aged man, yet here I go again.

I'm driving to Corvallis now. This period of solitude in the wee morning hours allows me time to think about why I again agreed to meet my wartime friends. It's been over twenty years since the first Gulf War and Operation Desert Storm. The three of us met in the military and because we were all Oregonians, quite naturally we gravitated toward each other. And we still feel a strong need to re-connect during this weeklong fishing vacation each year. The forest environment makes the differences in our current lifestyles melt, and we are able to relate to each other much as we did initially in 1991. Camping and fishing are activities not so far removed from our shared Marine Corps life back in the old days. However, combat, luckily, is no longer a part of our experience.

Corvallis is the town where my buddy, Billy Wright, landed after the war. It's a place where he would finish his college degree, fall in love, marry, and start what became a family of six.

With sandy blond hair that seems naturally in place no matter its length, style, or wind velocity, Billy looks forever a mischievous boy. His fast-moving eyes belie a delightfully devilish intent, yet his clean-shaven face, big smile, and good looks quickly endear him to each new acquaintance. He is what every mother would want for a son, yet fear in a son-in-law.

Always fun loving and sociable, Billy is well suited for his job as a new car salesman, the career he chose after he graduated college but before the babies came. Billy had never aspired to management positions or to business ownership and that was probably best because he found it difficult to work for any one dealership for more than two years. Initially, the car business was feast or famine, and that was exciting for him. I think Billy needs to constantly prove himself to himself, if to no one else. High self-esteem always seems fleeting to Billy which, I think, propels him onward to the next sale.

I often wondered if Billy's urge to move on was the result of Post-Traumatic Stress Disorder, or just a personality that relishes change. Although Billy regularly jumped jobs, his family has always remained stable because he never changed cities.

Always agreeable to a beer (and the occasional marijuana chaser) with friends and casual acquaintances, Billy has never walked away from a good time. I've often cautioned him as I watched his money flow toward fun and away from responsibilities, but his back-against-the-wall lifestyle just seems to motivate him toward another car sale.

Billy Wright could sell cars, and everyone in town knew it. Much like the country doctor who knows everyone because he delivered all the babies in the county, Billy had sold most families in Corvallis at least one car. He made money for whomever he worked and, although he was a sales maverick, he was highly valued by all the dealerships in town. Thanks to his business successes, his large family appreciated him. Although sometimes embarrassed by his antics, they certainly benefitted from his role of good provider and well-liked man about town. Billy is a fun-loving husband and father with a soft heart. Consequently, his occasional boyish wanderlust is accepted. I can't think of Billy without smiling myself. He isn't perfect, but he is a wartime friend who I will love always, not for his dependability, but for his optimism and love of life.

&

"Well, Twin, you're early as usual. In here, they're all still asleep so could you wait for me outside? I'll be with you in just a few."

"Billy, you're still an asshole—never on time. I even told you I'd be here a half an hour earlier than I planned to arrive, just to prevent this. I'll be in the truck. If I fall asleep, just load your stuff and then wake me. And come on, hurry, I don't want Chief waiting too long."

"Relax. I'm almost there. Is the back of the truck open?"

My Toyota 4Runner had a shell over the bed so all our gear would stay safe and dry. The plan was for Chief to meet us at the campsite. He'd be pulling a small trailer behind his Jeep Cherokee, as usual. The trailer would be full of wood and camp cooking equipment. Each of us were bringing our own tent, fishing gear, and snacks. Chief would bring food for meals to get us through at least half the week. For the rest, either Billy or I would make a run into the town of Enterprise for groceries. Enterprise, fifteen miles from the campground, catered to adventurers headed into the Eagle Cap Wilderness. The town specialized in the supplies we would need.

After more than ten years of taking this trip together, all three of us pitch in for meals and campsite chores and we've developed a system that needs very little pre-planning. We always head for the same river, same campsite, tell the same stories—and yet we look forward to this very same trip with eager anticipation.

"Goddamn, it's good to get on the road. I've been in Corvallis all summer and sure need a change of scenery and people. How you been, Twin?"

"Good as can be and as you know, I also work hard in the summer. Which is why, every September, you guys look pretty good to me. Shows you what kind of life I must have. Anyway, the weather for the week is supposed to be great. We should have no trouble getting into the Wallowas by late afternoon. We should probably call Chief to make sure he's on the road."

"If he leaves Portland in an hour, he'll still get there before us. You know Chief, he don't stop for nothing."

"Okay, Billy, if you keep me in coffee, I'll drive till lunch. And let me know when you have to take a leak. Otherwise kick back... and goddammit, Billy, put on your seatbelt."

The Eagle Cap Wilderness covers a rugged, primitive terrain in the majestic Wallowa Mountain Range in the northeast corner of Oregon. Rising out of the high plateau of eastern Washington and Oregon, and cut sharply by the Snake River Canyon on the east side, I believe these mountains are the most magnificent and remote in the country.

The Wallowa Mountains are often called the western Alps because its craggy mountaintops are scenically snow-capped most of the year. The crags were cut by glaciers and look like the teeth from a predatory, prehistoric, dinosaur jaw. The rugged terrain and raging rivers has discouraged the building of roads and structures, except for an occasional small wooden bridge. There is virtually nothing to indicate that humans exist beyond a few miles in, and no better hideout for those hoping to get lost for a while.

Years ago, we discovered a spot ideally suited for the three of us—tucked into a fold along the Lostine River. The river's source begins at Minam Lake, at 7,400 feet, and descends north out of the mountains on its journey, eventually linking up with the Snake River, which separates Oregon from Idaho.

On the north side of the range, the peaks jut up starkly, hiding in their shadows a gravel road that leads partway into the wilderness. As the road ascends, it follows the river and small, unimproved camping spots are cut into the forest every couple of miles. Some of the sites are designed for those who travel on horseback; other sites are large enough to accommodate more than one camp. Some even have a small outhouse. But none provides a source of fresh water, except direct from the river, of course.

Billy, Chief, and I have settled on a site nine miles up into the Wilderness, near the end of the gravel road, and more importantly, knee-deep in some of the best trout fishing in the state. By heading up there in September, we generally have the camp to ourselves and we've come to expect relatively good weather. The rain doesn't start until October, and that is followed by six months of snow.

I don't understand why other folks don't pick mid-September to head out for camping and fishing up there, but I'm careful never to advertise the spot. September is too late for summer vacationers and too early for the hunters. So I guess the mountains belong to us and, as Chief would say, the four-leggeds, the winged, and most importantly, the swimmers.

"Why don't we stop at the fly shop in Enterprise to find out what the fish are hitting on," Billy suggested as we neared the Lostine River. "Unlike you and Chief, I need all the help I can get."

"You shouldn't jinx yourself like that, Billy. Anyone who can sell cars like you can ought to be able to spot fish and reel them in. Isn't that what sales is all about? I know I couldn't land customers like you do. It's all the same technique—you've got to first believe you can, and then it seems to happen, right? Just visualize, Billy, visualize."

"Okay, Twin. How about if I visualize myself kicking your ass right now, before Chief gets here to save you? You're lucky he likes you so much. Sometimes I think he only tolerates me because of you. So I better kick your ass now."

"I should have said *fantasize* instead of visualize. You've always been great at fantasy," I laughed as I drove up to the fly shop.

Billy opened the wooden screen door and graciously allowed me to enter first. As I stepped by him, he planted his right foot into my aforementioned ass.

# Two: Stacey

"I CAN'T BELIEVE YOU PACKED A SUITCASE to go camping. You're so weird. Me and Mom just threw our things into boxes and a couple of backpacks."

Cody was talking to Harry, his younger cousin—younger by a mere six months. I recognized Cody's condescending putdown. My son has always been competitive with Harry. He says Harry has no camping experience at all. Which is probably true.

I guess I raised my oldest child to be the person I'd have liked to be if I were a boy. He has the perfect mix of looks and physique that my husband, Stanley Jones—who everyone calls "Coach"--and I could genetically provide. Cody is already six feet tall with my dark brown hair, dark brown eyes, and olive skin tone. He looks like the prince of McCall, Idaho. At least he does to me. He is popular with both boys and girls and although incurably lazy, Cody is my proudest accomplishment.

I have three other children—Julia, now an awkward 13-year-old; Olivia, the princess at 11; and our baby, Sir Lancelot, or just plain Lance, who is nearing the end of his eighth year. Cody is adept at positioning himself between his younger siblings and his parents—connected to us all, yet aloof.

If Cody's attitude toward Harry were something he could keep to himself, well, it wouldn't bother me. But he seems to want me to know that his cousin is inexperienced not only in camping, but in most other things as well. So it bothers me when I hear him gloat.

"I guess it don't matter much, but from where I come from, luggage doesn't fit into outdoor life at Eagle Cap Wilderness."

"This is all new to me," said Harry. "Maybe I should have called or texted you yesterday when we were packing. Mom and I were in the dark about what all to bring and Dad just pranced around bugging us about everything we took. But whatever—it'll be good to get out from under his thumb for a week. Just hope I won't be trading it for your screwed-up scrutiny."

Harrison Grimes is my brother's only child. I know he's been looking forward to this get-away with his mother, and with Cody and I—even if Cody sometimes sounds a lot like Harry's guilt-tripping dad. Our two high school graduates will be heading for the University of Idaho next month, and they decided to try their luck at rooming together in the freshman dorm, rather than trust their chances with strangers. So this week will be a good test run.

Harry is smaller than Cody—he's probably about five-foot-seven—and has a slight build. When I look at him, the word "ungainly" springs to mind. He seems to be a late bloomer, but I'm sure he'll fill out soon. Cody's black hair has a cowlick, and it seems to have been trimmed at home during a power failure. His face has a bad case of acne, but you almost don't notice because he has the most mesmerizing green eyes I've ever seen. Harry is a kid any aunt, such as myself, would love to hold and protect.

It's been years since the cousins spent extended time with each other, which is why my sister-in-law and I planned this end-of-summer camping trip. We figured the boys would have the chance to become better acquainted and it would give us adults quality time with our boys before they head off to the rest of their lives. Cynthia and I need this last unimpeded time with them. We figured the Wallowa Mountains would provide the ideal setting—far enough away from home, family, friends, and their ever-present social media obsessions.

Cynthia and Harry drove up to our place in McCall, Idaho, and left their sedan in my driveway. Then the four of us headed west to the Lostine River in northeastern Oregon. Cody's insistence on driving my SUV for the entire four-hour trip allowed the two teens to sit up front and appear years older as they plotted the course. Cynthia and I rode in back, in comfort, under the protection and control of our sons. I wondered why I'd never noticed before how mature they'd both become. I always thought they'd been tainted by their less-than-perfect fathers, and mothers who—I hate to admit it—settled into relationships that were far from ideal.

"We have two fairly large tents so why don't you two guys share one, and me and Aunt Cynthia will take the other," I said.

"Only if Harry agrees to leave his luggage in the car," said Cody. "I don't want my sleeping bag getting too close to this scientist from Boise. No telling what test tubes and microscopes he's brought along to clutter up the tent."

"All I'm bringing into the tent is my fishing gear, my knife, and my chewing tobacco," said Harry, glancing back at me then rolling his eyes.

I couldn't help but think how good it would be for Cody to be around his bright cousin. Growing up in McCall had afforded Cody all the advantages of an outdoor life that any child could hope for. Under his father's guidance, he'd learned that physical prowess and good muscular coordination would carry him far with his peers. And his excellent physique has helped to position him in good stead with the girls. Stanley, my husband, is an outdoorsy father. He's a popular teacher and the athletic mentor in Cody's high school and I'll be the first to admit that our reputation as parents has benefitted Cody.

McCall, Idaho, is a resort town where the locals know one another. Cody grew up with street credibility, which seems to have made the awkward teen years less so for him. His three younger siblings look up to him for leadership, which provides an environment for Cody to thrive. He's had the easiest course in life of anyone in my family. I suppose because things have always come easy for him, Cody has no noticeable anxieties. Everyone pays him a respect that he did very little to actually earn. I'll bet real money that kid will go far. Although I've never told him, Cody is my favorite person. And it gives me great comfort knowing Cody will have a full week of exposure to his cousin, Harry, who values education and seems career driven.

During a phone call when Cynthia and I were planning this trip, she confided her worry that Harry, an only child, has probably experienced too much motherly attention and not enough from his father, my brother Loren. Loren cares about Harry, of course, but he seems uncomfortable when spending time alone with him. Loren is a good provider, a hard-working employee and, although somewhat of a loner, has always placed his family first. Cynthia said Loren's interest in his family seems rooted in the belief that only he knows best.

Growing up, Loren was always quick to direct and oversee, but slow to participate. So it was good to hear Cynthia say that Harry seems to be a much more relaxed person than his dad is.

Loren met Cynthia when he was an accounting student at Boise State and she was a high school senior. Cynthia had deep roots in her church and parents who Loren respected. Although very attractive—in a clean and traditional way—Cynthia was not the type that caused young males to hunger for her. Her appearance was always understated, never flaunted.

Cynthia has black, short-cropped hair cut in a style usually reserved for older women. Her inexpensive clothing is utilitarian and uninspired. I knew it would be important for my brother to feel safe in her presence and Cynthia was intent on giving him no reason to doubt her loyalty. She's often told me how important it is to Loren that she never embarrass him. Consequently, she's grown into a stable and very accommodating wife who is not afraid of hard work or dirt.

What Loren desired he received, a woman of substance who kept the house clean and modeled righteous behavior, which made her attractive to the women of her church—but not to the men. Cynthia said she understood this dynamic in their relationship and was willing to play her role providing for her husband's comfort, both physically and emotionally. She balanced a family in ways that pleased Loren and provided a safe environment for their only child.

Cynthia also said that like his father, young Harry has few friends. However, unlike his father, his closest friends are independent intellectuals, and mostly female. Cynthia mentioned that Harry relates well to the girls due to their shared interests, in a non-sexual way that most other boys his age find difficult. I can assure you that he didn't get this attitude from his father, Loren, who has very definite gender barriers. Cynthia said that perhaps because Harry has relied so much on her, because he has no other siblings, and because he has such an agreeable personality, that he is more comfortable around females.

Cynthia said she used to worry that her son was gay. Nothing seemed to create as much anxiety and animosity among the women of her church as the fear that they were creating homosexual children. A homosexual lifestyle for her son, Cynthia admitted, was her most persistent fear and if it were true, it would create an insurmountable rift between father and son that would decimate her family.

At her husband's insistence, Cynthia's entire social life has revolved around church activities and the people in her congregation—a congregation that deplores any variance from traditional family structure. She describes herself as a homemaker who leaves her home for a portion of each day to do volunteer work for the pastor, much to the appreciation of both her husband and the pastor. So any hint of homosexuality from Harry would bring a fear of ruin and damnation upon her and the two males in her devoutly Christian home.

I told Cynthia I would watch Harry during this next week and let her know if I saw any hint of homosexual tendencies in my nephew. Even if he were gay, that would never affect my feelings for him. I'm not boasting when I say I have an uncanny ability to determine what motivates a man with regard to sexual energy. I don't know if that stems from my formative years living in a home awash in inappropriate male sexuality, or from living these past two and a half decades finely tuning my own sexual prowess. I've been blessed with good looks and enough sex appeal to find myself in many a situation where I've had to interpret male motivations.

Maybe Harry's comfort in befriending teenage girls has little to do with sexuality and more to do with personality and common interests, like Cynthia said. Then again, maybe not. However, I do get the impression that Harry is not as interested in male competition or dominance as Cody is. Harry seems focused on cooperation and global concerns. His sexual proclivities make little difference to me, but since Cynthia asked, I will observe. Assessment of male sexuality is perhaps my strongest talent.

"You know, Cody, I don't mind you telling me how to set up my side of the tent, but if you're going to mother me, I'm the wrong tent-mate. One mother is enough," said Harry. "And Aunt Stacey promised you would refrain from nagging."

"Touché," I said, overhearing Harry's comment. I cast a smile at Cynthia.

"Are we ever gonna decide on a campsite, or are we gonna spend the whole week driving on gravel?" asked our driver, Cody, as he maneuvered up the road along the Lostine River.

"This road can't go much further," said Cynthia. "It's been quite a way since we've seen any other cars. Have you noticed that the forest gets darker the deeper in we go?" said Cynthia in a weak voice from the backseat.

"We're fine, hon, especially with these big, smart college men. Let's drive on just a bit further," I said. I had a map open on my lap and was hoping that within a mile or two we'd find a campsite. I knew the boys appreciated my vote of confidence in them.

Cynthia views males differently than I do. I was raised with three brothers—Loren, who is older than me, and two younger brothers. Somehow, early on, I came to understand what interests men and proceeded to use that knowledge to promote my own goals. Men have egos that constantly need stroking, which means I show all the men in my life that *they* are my personal favorite. All of them, that is, except Loren. I discovered that a coy personality works well with most men. Loren is one of the exceptions. He saw me as a threat to his role as the oldest child, and has ruthlessly competed with me every possible way since I was born. Realizing his game, and the importance he placed on winning, I put up no resistance to his animosity, which further infuriates him.

Loren met Cynthia at church, and with what seemed to me to be very little effort on his part, they courted for an appropriate amount of time before they married. His accomplishments did more for their marriage than any loving behavior from him. I can't imagine that tender words or gestures of affection flowed from him. But he was a college student from a stable god-fearing family, and showed promise. Loren must have seemed like a good choice for Cynthia and her family. No one paid attention to the fact that he had no friends. It was weird that he was so all-consumed with his studies that he showed little interest in anything beyond his new girlfriend.

Loren and Cynthia were married on an altar in a church-sanctioned ceremony, and the couple quickly settled into roles dictated by my brother. Cynthia's role was to provide a male child to solidify Loren's legacy, and once that had been accomplished, he seemed satisfied, and she seemed relieved. After that, Cynthia whispered to me, their sex life diminished.

Harrison Grimes was baptized immediately upon leaving the hospital and the child became the focus of Cynthia's attention. This suited Loren's vision of family life. Discussions of family business had no place in church or community, so Cynthia's occasional conversations with me were a major outlet for her. As her sister-in-law, I became the conduit that allowed her to report and receive news about the extended Grimes family. I guess I was the person most willing to talk with her, and I was compassionate when she voiced concerns about her relationship with Loren. Even though my brother discouraged communication between Cynthia and me, she protected and valued our sisterly bond. Our conversations provided a counter-balance to the unconditional praise she and her family received from their church fellowship.

Loren has been an accountant in the Boise State University administration for the past twenty years, and an alderman in their church. Cynthia told me she believed that her marriage was blessed and that therefore she had little room to complain. But I've occasionally advised her not to lose herself. I've pointed out many times that she has left herself little room to flourish as an individual because Loren makes all the family decisions.

Well, most of the decisions that is, except for a big, recent one. Against Loren's wishes, and after a strong case made by his normally compliant son, Loren reluctantly agreed to Harry's selection of Idaho State University in Moscow, Idaho, as his college of choice. Loren had hoped to see Harry attend the fine local university where he was employed, but Harry said he'd feel stifled at Boise State for exactly that reason. Harry was adamant about attending Idaho State and Cynthia supported that decision. So, Loren grudgingly gave in.

And this past June, Cynthia called to tell me that Loren was allowing her and Harry to spend a week in September with me and Cody. I'd never heard her so happy. I knew Loren had reservations about letting them spend time with me because he accused me of intimidating him.

Loren said I am certainly in league with the devil and a bad influence on his wife. But that there was probably not much trouble his wife and son could get into while isolated on the Lostine River. I think he also had to admit that a week of camping would be beneficial for the boys. He said he trusted that the focus of our week would be on college and the boys' bonding, not on my flamboyant and irresponsible lifestyle practiced in that hedonistic town of McCall, Idaho.

"HERE WE GO. HOW'S THIS PLACE LOOK?" asked Cody. "There's plenty a room and no one else is here." He turned the car off the gravel road, passed through a stand of Ponderosa pines and tall fir, then drove past a small outhouse. Off to the right was a cleared patch of ground covered with pine needles. There was a picnic table and plenty of space for tents on both sides of a large fire pit.

"Home sweet home," I said. "As long as you guys don't mark this site by pissing anywhere nearby."

"I'm ready to be done with this car," said Harry. "So I say let's call this good." He opened his door and stepped out before anyone else moved.

Because there was no reason to say no, the rest of us got out of the car and began setting up our camp. The boys carried our gear and supplies to the heavy wooden picnic table while Cynthia and I designated areas for our tents, chairs, and food prep equipment. We decided the tent that the boys would share should be placed on one side of the table and fire pit, and the mothers' tent would be directly across from them. We figured having the fire pit in between us would provide sufficient separation and privacy.

Cody and Harry agreed to set up both tents while Cynthia and I began to unpack the boxes of equipment and food, spreading out everything on the picnic table. It was an idyllic setting, but soon our attention was diverted by the sound of an automobile's tires leaving the gravel and winding through the trees toward us.

"Just what we need—company," whined Cynthia.

"But it looks like just one man. Why don't you boys go see what he wants?"

"Can we help you with anything?" Cody asked the man as he drove close in a battered Jeep Cherokee pulling a small trailer. Harry was right by Cody's side.

"Are you just arriving, or breaking camp?" the man asked.

From what I could see, he was a good-looking, middle-aged guy with a long, black ponytail. He had high cheekbones and several leather wristbands on hands that continued gripping his steering wheel. His face was rugged and obviously Native American.

"I plan to set up a camp over in that group of trees to the left of you, and I'm expecting two friends who should be right behind me."

"We just got here ourselves," Cody told him. "There's four of us, but that other site leaves us all with plenty of room—if you don't mind sharing the outhouse."

"These two ladies are our mothers," Harry said. "Cody and I are cousins."

*Too much information for a stranger?* I wondered. Curious, I approached. "There are plenty of other spots up and down the river. But we've already unpacked so it would be too much trouble for us to leave."

Unfortunately, the stranger didn't take my hint. "My two friends and I have been coming to this spot for years and we like to fish in certain holes along this stretch of river. They expect me to begin setting up the camp before they arrive and might not find me if I go somewhere else. My name is Ben Troxler and I work for the Oregon Department of Fish and Wildlife. I know all these rivers and most of the trails leading from them. I think you'll find us to be pretty quiet guys who spend almost all daylight hours on the river fishing and then go to sleep as soon as it gets dark."

"We plan to fish too," said Cody. "Do you think you could turn us on to the best trout holes? We haven't gotten down to the river yet but we plan to spend a lot a time there. I'm sure there's plenty a water for us all."

It seemed Cody had already accepted Ben and the idea that his two friends would be joining him. In order to show that I, too, could be a good neighbor, I said, "We have no problem sharing this site with you, Ben. There's plenty of room over at that other campsite. Why not send your friends over to meet us once they've settled in?"

With no change of expression or words of agreement, Ben Troxler put his Jeep into gear and drove to the campsite fifty yards away.

I turned, morphed my face into a noticeable frown, and walked back to the picnic table to let Cynthia know we would not be completely alone.

# Three: Twin

"GOOD WORK CHIEF. Glad you were able to get our usual spot," I said, glancing over at the SUV with Idaho plates. "Have you met our neighbors?"

"Yeah, they got here right before me. They seem nice—two mothers and two teenage boys. Didn't ask how long they plan to stay"

Chief, known as Ben Troxler in his real life, snuck up behind Billy and gave him a huge bear hug that lifted him off his feet. "You'll have to watch that foul mouth of yours. I don't want those women getting on our case."

"If you don't let go of me, they'll hear stuff that would most likely send them packing fast for Idaho," Billy said.

It's never taken the three of us long to pick up our friendship right where we left off. Nothing much has changed about that for more than twenty years. And it took no time at all for us to unload and set up camp.

I could hear the Idaho group still discussing where to put things as we donned waders and assembled our poles in a race to see who could get to the river first.

Our two campsites are about twenty yards in from the river and each has a well-defined path leading down to the water. The trees and undergrowth are so thick that I can hear the water flowing, but can't see it from camp. In fact, outside of the camp clearing it is hard to see beyond the immediate trees. The tall pine, spruce, and fir, with their subtle variations of green, keep out the heat and brightness of the sun. The ground is covered with the tree's soft needles, and beams of diffused light filter eerily through the high branches.

So the campsites remain cool even in the heat of the day. And even though the two mothers and their kids over there are so close, they're barely visible. I like the privacy.

Chief reached the river first, as always. He'll likely be the last to return. For him, fly-fishing is not a hobby or work. It's a lifestyle that dictates most of his decisions. Forever a bachelor, Chief identified and quickly obtained a job in his chosen career right after his discharge from the military. He went to only one potential employer, was hired immediately, sent to college by the Department of Fish and Wildlife, and spent these last twenty years amply satisfied. He says the best aspect of his job with the department is that it provides him with the personal pleasure of river exploration and a hands-on reconnaissance of the plentiful inventory of rivers in his native state of Oregon.

Chief explained that he'd been tasked with improving native fish habitat, and that the job begins with walking or boating thousands of miles of river. He is proud that his findings have helped to initiate the laws that help manage native fish populations with the goal of becoming self-sustainable while allowing for recreational and, in some cases, commercial fishing.

Over the last decade, the state constructed numerous fish hatcheries, which has helped sustain the numbers of fish for recreational fishing, but Chief's goal has always been to improve the number of native fish. He has often told us that farmed hatchery fish is just a temporary solution, not an end goal. As one of a team of scientist-outdoorsman who explore the state, Chief reports on his observations and makes recommendations. Suggested fishing limits and improvement of habitat are his areas of expertise, but he leaves enforcement of the law to others. Chief describes himself as primarily an avid fly fisherman paid to scout out the best spots and to ensure a healthy fishery for the next year and beyond.

"You know, Twin, it doesn't surprise me that Chief always catches the biggest and most fish. He gets on the river first and fishes the best stretch for himself," groaned Billy.

"We could have been here first if you'd been ready when I got to Corvallis. Besides, you and I need an excuse for our smaller catch."

In truth, fishing, for me, has always been an excuse to come to places like this. Any fish I catch is secondary to the place I catch them.

"Okay. So, once again it's all my fault," Billy said. "By the way, did you happen to see what kind of fly he tied on?"

"Knowing Chief, it was a dry fly," I replied. "Probably some sort of caddis. That's what I'm planning to start with. If the fish aren't rising, I'll switch to a streamer or nymph."

"I'm gonna head upstream from Chief," said Billy. "When I pass him, I'll check out what he's using and see if they're rising. See you about an hour before dark for dinner."

# Four: Stacey

"IT'S A GOOD THING you thought to have us stop to buy Oregon fishing licenses in that last town we passed," said Harry. "Who would have thought we would be camped next to some official fishing guy. Do you know what the rules are here and everything like that?"

Cody was rigging his pole to begin fishing. "I don't think he's a cop, but if you're not sure about something, just ask that guy. He seems nice enough and he's probably just upriver from us. The clerk at the store said not to use bait, but he didn't mention any limits or stuff like that. I think we're good to go."

"Let me see what you plan to use. You fish a lot around McCall and probably the same kind of lures would work here. I'll watch you get started."

"Your dad doesn't fish much, does he, Harry? Do you and your friends in Boise fish at all?" asked Cody.

I was eavesdropping on the boys' exchange and

guessed Cody already knew the answer to his question.

Recently, Cody admitted to me that he figured he'd need to rely on Harry's greater experience in all things related to schoolwork. He'd never been much interested in his education, but said he realized that would have to change in college. Good study habits are not Cody's strong suit, despite growing up under the roof of a teacher. He's preferred to rely more on his dad's athletic coaching knowledge and his father preferred the same. Completion of his schoolwork had always been left for me to oversee, which never made any sense to me since my own performance in high school was abysmal.

I'm not sure how it happened, but even I call Stanley, my husband, "Coach." I suppose Coach is more descriptive than personal, but it defines where our relationship has gone over time. He is an ultra busy and aloof man. I have allowed him to leave all family business to me. What I do benefits the others in most ways, but not with regard to Cody's schoolwork. Never a motivated student myself, I feel deficient in supervising my children's work.

Cody told me his goal in rooming with Harry was to observe and imitate his cousin's study skills, and that although he preferred to become a better student through osmosis, he knew that wasn't likely. Cody seems less anxious about his performance in college knowing Harry will be close by. He may not want to hang out socially with Harry, but facing the dreaded burning of the midnight oil, who better to have as an ally than his studious cousin?

Cynthia said Harry's only worry about college is how his departure will affect her. They both figure that Loren, a solitary, difficult man to live with, will adjust just fine.

Loren has always been strongly opinionated and quick to cast negative judgment about anyone outside the family. He is derisive of people at work, at church, and especially the stifling government. He's elected himself gatekeeper for the family and sees this as a noble role. He acts as if his vigilant oversight keeps his family safe and successful. The slightest hint of disrespect—real or imagined--is a threat that must be overcome. Loren's style of retribution is subversive, passive-aggressive. The recipient may not even notice. Cynthia said Harry worries she will be too vulnerable to Loren's aggressive rigidity when he heads off to college, leaving her alone.

The way I see it, Cynthia and Harry have been complying with my brother's every wish as if it were the glue keeping their family together. They are the sounding board to his anger, deflecting and absorbing it in a way that keeps him above public reproach.

I'm on Harry's side about this issue. I, too, wonder if Cynthia will be strong enough to withstand her burden alone.

When Cynthia and I were initially planning this trip, she said Harry was all for the idea that the retreat be just for the two moms and two boys. Harry told her, 'Dad would just say, "A retreat for what purpose?" Everyone requires change, but not Dad. He's just not interested in the topic. I want this camping trip in Oregon with you, Mom, to provide enough memories to carry you along until I return for the winter holidays.'

I was happy to hear this report from Cynthia.

Harry is fortunate that his mother taught him the skills required to identify, comply with, and adjust to a strong personality. I couldn't have taught anyone that. Cody will probably take on a persona much like Coach's, but Harry is good at accepting instruction and complying with commands. Following orders doesn't seem to cause him any stress or resentment.

&

"Get that line in the water so we can bring our moms some dinner," Cody called out to Harry. "I figure it'll take about six to eight good-size trout to satisfy us. My appetite is big when camping, so get your shiniest lure into the water."

"God, it sure is nice to get away," I said to Cynthia. "We've all been too busy to connect these last few years.

But with Harry and Cody in school together, I assume we will see more of each other. At least I hope we do. I'm so glad that Harry can deal with Cody. I know my kid can be pompous and set in his ways, but he really does appreciate Harry even though he doesn't show it. Does Loren still refuse to call him anything but Harrison?"

"Pretty much," said Cynthia. "Loren thinks of his son as a future attorney and Harry is too common a name. Too folksy."

"Both names fit him well. There's two sides to his character," I said. "Aristocrat, and the guy next door. I love Harry and I'm so glad we have this week together."

"Actually," said Cynthia. "I think Harry will benefit more from sharing a dorm room with Cody because he's grown up an only child and always hoped for a brother. Although Harry and I spend a lot of time together, that's not the same as a close male friend. This trip is such a good idea for so many reasons."

"I'm sure the boys will have no problem leaving us and heading out on their new adventure, but I'll miss my son. I'm glad I'm not letting go of him alone—I have you to talk with, and hopefully the boys will have each other."

Cynthia and I looked at each other and I know a tear crept into my eye. I got up and gave Cynthia a hug, the first one we'd shared in several years.

The cool cleanliness and fresh fragrance of an evergreen forest more than compensates for the lack of color change during the Pacific Northwest's fall season. The pungent pine needles that carpet the ground lends a softness and comfort to the raw majesty of the eighty-foot-tall trees and powerful river flowing nearby. As dusk approached, I paused to appreciate the surroundings and allowed nature to envelope me as it pulled its curtain on the day. Such a welcome change to my normal routine at home. I could hear the three men campers next door heading back in to their campsite too.

Prior to leaving home, Cynthia and I had planned the dinner menus. We'd both packed ingredients to make a few meals and had agreed to jointly prepare the food. We were two moms adept at feeding our sons.

So, our camp settled in to building a fire and making dinner. Without any prompting, Cody pitched in, helping in ways he would never think of at home. The conversation was easy and relaxed. We caught up on news, and sometimes no one talked at all.

"We both did pretty well," said Cody. "But the fish were mostly small and not worth keeping. But once Harry got the hang of it, he really seemed to get into it and I saw him haul in a few."

Cynthia stopped cutting carrots, and with a beaming smile asked, "How many, Harry?"

"Well, I hooked six but landed only four. I saw one of our neighbors catch some really good-sized fish. He was just up river from me and using a fly pole. Those guys get right into the water and wade up and down the river. They don't miss a thing. They can get to places Cody and I can't. By moving along in the water and with a delicate finesse, a guy can cast his line and have it land right where he wants it to. These movements looked beautiful to me."

"Harry," I said as I walked by him and flicked his baseball cap off his head, "if you're going to be a fisherman, you're going to have to learn how to exaggerate your ass off."

"I'm so proud of you, Harry," his mother said.

"What about me?" said Cody. "I caught a bunch of fish too!"

"That's what I mean about exaggeration, Harry," I said and winked at my son.

The boys took on the responsibility of maintaining the fire and they ate what we served without any negative feedback.

# Five: Twin

"I'VE ALWAYS THOUGHT DEER were the most graceful animal that moves through the woods but when I saw that woman in the next camp walking to the head, I changed my mind," said Billy. "She is so hot that I couldn't keep from staring. Have you guys seen her yet?"

"Slow down, Billy," Chief said. "I talked to them on my way in and they look like decent folks who didn't come here looking to party with someone like you. The women seemed disappointed that we would be sharing this campground with them, but I told them that we fish all day and sleep at night. Let's keep it that way. Okay?"

"Am I right or what, Twin?" asked Billy, looking for some agreement.

"You horn-dog," I said. "Don't you ever slow down? It doesn't surprise me that you can find a woman even in the wilderness, but I've seen her too and in this case, you're right. She's very attractive. But remember where you are now and where you just came from."

Chief nodded in agreement. "Twin's right on, Billy. I saw the boys fishing on the bank this afternoon. They seem like nice kids who politely gave me all the room I needed. They'll probably stay close to their camp and not realize there are better fishing spots further along the river. Anyway, Billy, why don't you and Twin walk over and introduce yourselves. Twin will make sure you don't obnoxiously hit on the women."

"I'm not planning to hit on anyone. But I sure don't mind looking."

&

"Hi! Did you guys do any good today on the river?" I asked as I walked through the forest separating our campsite from the moms and sons. "We figured we'd better come over and introduce ourselves."

"Not bad," said Cody. "I don't know if we're using the best lures. Are they hitting on your flies?"

"Our flies are probably not as enticing as what you're using. What makes it fun is the lengths we go to trying to outsmart the fish," I said. "And judging by the results, most often they figure us out first."

"Are you guys all with Fish and Game?" asked the pretty lady.

I have to admit that Billy was right. She doesn't look

old enough to have a grown child. She sure is striking—in a naturally athletic way. Her thick shoulder-length hair and green eyes frame a smile that, without a doubt, could pierce the rough skin of the toughest stranger. If she's not an athlete, she must be a dancer.

"No, just one of us is a Fish and Game guy," Billy said. "Twin and I are just a couple of civilians who like fishing and camping. We've known each other since our time serving in the military, and we get together once a year, at that spot over there, and spend the week catching up. Again, I'm Billy Wright and this is Ken Morrison, who we call Twin, and the guy you met earlier is Chief."

"Well, I guess we'll be neighbors this week. I'm Stacey Lee Jones," the good-looking one said. Then she introduced us to Cynthia, the other mother, and Harry.

Stacey seems more sociable than Cynthia, who remained standing behind Harry, seated at the picnic table. Neither of them said a word. Harry must be her son, and neither seem inclined to open up to strangers in remote settings.

"Let us know if there's anything we can help with," I said, trying to ease their discomfort. "Folks often forget to pack things and we'd be happy to share. By the way, I see you brought water bottles. If you run out of water, don't drink river water even though it looks clean. Fill a pot of water from the river and bring it to our campsite. Run it through our purifier. It'll be much better for you."

"It's nice of you to offer that, and we might have to take you up on it. It'll be nice not to have to ration what we brought," Stacey replied. "We'll need to go to town to re-supply at some point. We'll especially need firewood, and we'd be happy to pick up something if you need it, too."

"Sounds like a deal," I said. "Come on, Billy. Let's let them get back to whatever they were doing."

# Six: Stacey

AFTER THE MEN LEFT, HARRY SAID, "They seem like nice guys. Like they respect our privacy."

"Anybody who can speak that highly of a fish, about how smart the fish actually are, is probably not a brute," I said, looking at Cynthia. "I think they'll be just fine as neighbors."

"I just hope we don't meet up at the outhouse in the middle of the night," Cynthia replied.

"Aw, Ma," Harry groaned. "Guys don't use the outhouse at night. The fact is, we don't get very far from our tent."

"Listen to Harry! I didn't know he was such an experienced camper," said Cody. "Does he pee in the backyard at home in Boise, Aunt Cynthia?"

I was happy to see Cynthia scowl at my son.

# Seven: Twin

WE SETTLED IN TO EATING OUR DINNER, followed by the most relaxing couple of hours of any day—hoisting a few around a campfire. The one detriment of drinking beer is the middle-of-the-night struggles with sleeping bag zippers, tent zippers, and stumbling far enough into the forest so as not to befoul our camp. All done with the hope of remaining half-asleep.

"You're right, Chief," I said. "Those people are nice. I offered them use of our water purifier. I think they saw some sense to it."

"One of the women didn't seem sure of us, but the good-looking one is cool," reported Billy.

"The other one is not bad looking. She just looks more her age. The one you like seems younger than she probably is. Anyway, they're mothers, just like our wives."

"Are you saying that when I get up tonight to take a leak, I shouldn't wander off in their direction?"

"Right," I said. "And not in my direction either."

# Eight: Stacey

"THE FIRST NIGHT OF CAMPING always feels best," Cody said as the two teens crawled into their tent. "My sleeping bag is so comfy, especially with the new air cushion. Mom used to put us in blankets right on the ground when I was a kid. This is like sleeping at home."

Cody and Harry arranged their sleeping bags with space between them for clothing and gear. We didn't expect visits from bear or wolf, but one can never be sure in these mountains. I hadn't said anything about food attracting wildlife, but Cody put all the grocery bags and coolers back in the SUV. Harry put the table scraps in a bag and stored that in the car as well. They did good!

Cynthia and I chatted long after the boys went to bed. We could hear their voices, but not what they said. I'm sure they appreciated their moms close, but not too close. We needed the same privacy. I couldn't hear voices coming from the men's camp. I assume they retired early.

# Nine: Cody

WE WERE IN OUR TENT with flashlights on and I saw Harry paging through the Idaho State University course catalogue. Although catalogues are available online, it was smart for Harry to print out a copy for us. Now we can research classes while on vacation, without Wi-Fi access.

"Have you decided yet on the classes you're gonna take?" I asked Harry. "I hope none of them start too early in the morning."

"I'm just getting prepared. I was told the best classes get filled early and I thought I'd better get a head start while on this trip. It would be good for both of us to go through this, not necessarily tonight, but sometime before we get to the college. We might want to take some classes together. "

"I've heard the same advice. It's good that you brought the catalogue. I'd have probably gotten to school empty handed, but I hope you'll give me the push I need—just not tonight, I mean. Okay, Harry?"

"I pretty much know what classes I want to take."

"I have some idea of what I want, too, but I'm likely to put off the decisions until the last minute and then do it only half-assed. I get frustrated with planning out stuff. It's like I find other things to do that are more fun, so I just do them. Harry, if you'll help me get my course schedule worked out, I'd feel better about our first week at school. If I can get by that week, I know I'd have a chance at catching the groove. Everyone says college will be an adventure, so any prep I do now will help me get into the adventure part sooner."

"I'll be glad to help you pick your classes this week," offered Harry.

"Great! Harry, I'm interested in what classes you're planning to take and, kidding aside, I can probably handle it if some are scheduled for early in the morning."

"Sounds good. You mentioned that you haven't chosen a major yet, and that's cool. But you're required to take some courses necessary for graduation no matter what your major. My plan is to get them out of the way early."

"You really believe you're gonna graduate someday?" I asked.

"That's the goal, isn't it? Otherwise what are we going to college for?"

"Harry, if you'll just remind me of that from time to time, you'll be the perfect roomie for me. I get so caught up in sports, girls, and partying that I forget what I'm supposedly heading for. If you help me stay focused on graduating, I'll do my part and fix you up with some dates."

"Whatever, Cody. I'm not sure we have the same taste in women," Harry said.

# Ten: Stacey

WHEN CYNTHIA AND I ARRANGED the inside of our tent, we placed our air mattresses and sleeping bags in the middle, and put our clothing and necessities around the outside perimeter. The boys were still talking softly when we let the fire die down and headed to bed. I was delighted to hear their voices because it meant there is a good possibility they will form a friendship that could sustain them through four years of college.

"They seem to be getting along just great," I said to Cynthia.

"Do you think you'll miss Cody when he leaves?"

"Of course I will," I said. "But I suspect it will be easier for me than for you. My other kids will still keep me busy and I don't expect much change around the house. Since Harry is your only child, I imagine his departure will leave a huge emptiness."

"But what about Cody? Do you think he'll miss your family?"

"Cody has always been very active after school. He's gone out for all the sports teams, never with great success—but he's been a good teammate. And he's always had lots of friends, and lately, friends who are girls. In fact, he's spent more time at his girlfriend's house this summer than at ours. So, no, I don't think he'll miss us much," I said. "Cody said the girlfriend is jealous that he chose to spend this week with his mother. I think he wants her to get a message he doesn't want to deliver in person. He seems to be starting to cut the emotional ties, and I can't say that I blame him. He said she's become clingy. But, back to your question, I think Cody will do just fine."

As I said all this, I realized that Cody is probably more emotionally prepared for this departure than I am.

"I think you're right," said Cynthia. "I'm so glad Harry chose to spend this week with me and you two. But I'm not prepared to let him go yet. We hang around together a lot because he has only a few friends and rarely goes out. We've had our set routines, but now all that will change and I'm worried about how my life will be the moment he walks out the door. Most of my conversations with Loren have to do with Harry, so I'm not sure we'll have anything to talk about now. I'll miss Harry terribly much."

Loren and I have had scant contact since we both left home. Loren is a pompous, angry asshole, just like our father. By my late teens, I had decided to stop putting up with Dad's rage, and moved into the home of my closest friend. Getting out from under the thumb of Loren was also a relief. The only reason I have a relationship with Loren now is because we have to get along for the sake of our families. We're polite to each other, but we keep our distance. If it weren't for Cynthia, I would probably have no contact with Loren at all.

Lying here next to Cynthia, makes me think about my disturbing history with her husband. Loren has always disliked me, perhaps just being born and taking attention away from him as a baby set the stage for all that happened later. I played a hateful game of revenge when I reached high school and his friends started showing more interest in me than they did in him. Loren and I were only one grade apart, and some of his friends made little secret about the reason they hung around our house. I remember the moment Loren realized I was the reason he had friends at all.

From that point on, Loren made my life miserable. But I chose to do nothing to ease my older brother's loss of esteem—it was my way of paying him back. I cultivated my ability to charm his friends. Attracting and manipulating those young men became even easier as my shape morphed into something more womanly and their interest in Loren stopped as soon as he provided them with an introduction to me.

Loren called me a vamp, even in relation to our father. He left evidence of my supposed escapades—all fantasies designed by him—around the house to get me in trouble. But I never tried to repudiate his attempts to besmirch my reputation, and that just incensed him more.

I had no interest in entering Loren's imaginary world because I was more focused on reality. His only accusations that had an element of truth were those that linked me with my father. Not true, however, were his insinuations that I initiated sexual behavior with Dad. What actually occurred between my father and me was even more sordid than Loren's imagination conjured up.

"Cynthia, are you still awake?"

"Yes, Stacey."

"I want you to know that I haven't always loved my brother, but I was really happy for him when you two met and decided to marry. I knew that having you in his life would be great for him. You seemed unselfish and such a decent human being, as well as having an immense strength of character. You seem to focus on Loren's best traits. I just wanted you to know how much I appreciate you and I regret never saying this to you before. I probably wouldn't have any relationship with Loren today if it were not for you and Harry."

"Thank you, Stacey. That means a lot to me. Sleep well."

As I listened to Cynthia's breathing slow down and become rhythmical, my thoughts returned to Loren. He and I grew up disliking each other and that was probably because we were too close in age, which led to competition between us, especially over friends. Because he was a boy, Loren was the focus of our dad's attention. Dad just didn't know how to bond with a daughter. He tried, but in ways that were just plain wrong. He must have known only one way to show love to a female, but because I was his daughter—and a child—what he did was totally inappropriate.

I thought of my father as a touchy, feely parent, but realized later that he was just twisted and what he did to me would be considered criminal, abusive behavior. I would report him to the police if he were still alive, to ensure he wouldn't abuse anyone ever again. Dad tried to engage with me physically, as if I was forever a baby to cuddle, but as I reached school age, I stopped allowing his caresses. I began to defend myself. He couldn't understand what he called my 'coldness,' and so he just wrote me off and ignored me. I'm glad my parents had no additional daughters. Consequently, I spent my early years learning what it was that males want and how far they will go to get it.

My father's physical abuse of me and the lack of good adult direction made it impossible for me to feel close to my brother. I never gave Loren a chance. I kept my distance from him and deliberately used his friends as a wedge between us. After high school, I went my own way and never looked back. But in some strange ways, I've always loved them both. Maybe the sickness lies in me—I don't really know. But I always hoped they would both find happiness. I think Loren eventually did, when he met Cynthia.

Just then, Cynthia turned over in her sleeping bag and out of the blue said, "I've always thought religious differences caused the breakdown between you and Loren and your parents."

"That's part of it, I'm sure," I said.

"Well just so you know that you're now my sister and I love you. And so does Harry," Cynthia said. She rolled over and went back to sleep.

# Eleven: Cody

"ARE YOU STILL A VIRGIN?" I asked Harry.

"That's pretty personal, but since you're my cousin, yeah, I guess so."

"That cracks me up," I laughed. "What do you mean, 'I guess so?' You either are or aren't; there's no in-between."

"I did get a hand job by a girl for whom I helped set up a Facebook page. Does that count?"

Trying to stifle a laugh that made it hard to form words, I said, "For Facebook, you should have gotten more. You're giving away your work too cheap, Harry. But don't worry; I'll help you remedy that. We'll get you laid before freshman year is up."

"I can take care of myself, thank you. But I am glad that you're going to be my roommate."

"Yeah, it'll be a kick. We'll start off as low men on the totem pole but I think we'll make a good team," I yawned. "Goodnight, Harry."

# Twelve: Twin

I OPENED MY EYES, but continued lying still in my sleeping bag. It was almost dawn. Within ten minutes, both Chief and Billy crawled out of their tents and quietly addressed the morning's three important tasks: start brewing coffee, rekindle yesterday's fire, and stroll to the outhouse. In that order. We've finely tuned this choreographed routine so no one had to speak.

One at a time, we made our way to the fire. Once the coffee was good to drink, we started bantering about the fish. By then, the sun had risen high enough to provide enough light for us to head for the river. Each day begins with the hope that we'll choose our fishing spots well.

Much like the racetrack tout who researches the horses, racing conditions, and past performances prior to deciding where to place his last two-dollar bet, we fishermen do our own obsessive mental contortions hoping to ensure our success on the river. Later on, we'll rationalize and justify our decision to the others. For me, the expectation of the catch is the best part. I choose a new site every day.

This Lostine River flows swiftly in spots, which means it moves too fast for safe footing of both human and fish. Neither wants to work too hard; neither wants to fight the current just to stay put. Slow-moving water is ideal. A pocket of water just behind a fast-moving stretch makes it easier for the trout to sit tight and let the food flow past at a relaxed, steady speed.

A river travels slower along the bank. Over-hanging vegetation above, and rocks and plants below, provides a better level of protection than the middle. I hope to enter the river and then work my flies from the middle to the slower moving pools on the far bank. If shallow enough, I can work both sides while moving up and down river, and attempting to not get my line snagged in the trees.

Billy and Chief will be doing the same thing, most likely out of sight, but not far from me.

The three of us have a keen appreciation of this pristine scenery, mixed with a bit of our own unique brand of superstition. We're all looking for a stretch of water that "speaks to us."

The most important aspect of a successful fishing day is sufficient early morning light. We typically fish for about three hours after having our morning coffee, then return to camp for breakfast and for bragging about our morning.

Depending on the heat at midday, we might choose to stay dry in camp until the sun indicates it is late afternoon. We spend those hours talking, reading, napping, or making the forty-five minute drive into town. But by late afternoon, we again don our waders and vests and head out to fish until an hour before dark.

# Thirteen: Harry

"THOSE GUYS GET UP PRETTY EARLY, I could hear their fire going around daybreak," I said to Cody when he began stretching and peeked outside the tent.

"You think they would mind if we took a log from their fire to get ours going? We didn't bring nearly as much wood as we need and it's pretty nippy out here. Why don't you go over there and get us a log, Harry, and we'll get this place warm for our moms."

"Not me. What if they come back and see me poking around their camp? I don't want to be shot for stealing a burning log. You do it."

"All right, puss. Then we'll just have to start the fire the hard way."

From inside the women's tent came a plaintive moan, "Is there any coffee yet?"

"Mom, go back to sleep," said Cody. "We're just starting a fire and we'll make coffee, but you'll wake

Aunt Cynthia if you don't stop whining. I'm not like Dad who has everything ready for you in the morning."

"Trouble is, you're too much like me," Stacey called out. After a pause she said, "Harry! Don't you let him make you do all the work!"

# Fourteen: Stacey

"GO BACK TO SLEEP," I heard Cody call out. Cynthia opened her eyes and began laughing.

I was glad the men from the other campsite had already left, leaving us unimpeded access to the rustic bathroom facilities. Calling the outhouse a bathroom, and even using the term rustic, is a compliment to the tiny closet that holds a wooden bench over a hole in the dirt. I guess it's better than nothing at all.

"Want to use the powder room first?" I offered my sister-in-law.

"Be my guest, and while you're at it chase off the animals that are using it for shelter."

Our first breakfast, like our first dinner, was not well planned. But with quiet politeness, Cynthia and I worked in tandem. We surveyed the supplies and devised a menu. I was particularly mindful of not making assumptions as we negotiated our way through the preparation of scrambled eggs, diced potatoes, and sausage, which became the perfect camp breakfast when all piled on a single plate.

We all sat on folding chairs around the fire. Our living room walls were forest trees. Pine needles made up our floor. Diffuse sunlight shafted its way down to us, and the fresh and musty smell of the evergreens made the spot magnificent. Harry and Cody both said it was the best breakfast they'd ever eaten.

"Do you guys plan to fish this morning?" I asked the boys. "If that's your plan, why don't you get started because Aunt Cynthia and I plan to hike one of these trails this afternoon and we'd love to have you both join us."

"Until we get to know our way around here better, I think it would be nice for us all to explore, together," added Cynthia.

Being in a remote place with no one in sight except three strange men is something Cynthia would never have chosen for herself, so I figured if she became more familiar with the area, she'd be less anxious about camping in the wild.

"All right, we'll go too," Harry said. "But you can hardly get lost with the river running north/south through everything and the road running along the river. How about you, Cody? Does that sound good to you? Fishing and then hiking."

"Sounds like a plan to me."

# Fifteen: Cody

"HAVING ANY LUCK?" I called out to the campsite stranger named Billy.

"Not much today," Billy called back. "Are you wanting to fish here?"

"Not necessarily. I'm just looking for a good spot and it's a big river. You three headed out early, but we had a great breakfast first."

"You're lucky to have moms that can tend to that stuff. Not that I'm a chauvinist or anything, but it sure helps to have that female touch. Do you guys have dads too?"

"Oh, yeah, but my dad works, and my younger sisters and brother stayed home this time. Harry's dad isn't into camping and fishing. My mom, Stacey, thought up the idea of just taking a trip for the mothers and sons. Harry and I are heading off to college and this is kind of like the last hurrah. Harry spends a lot of time with his mom, but me and my mom are both busy and we don't spend much time together. But she's a real cool mom."

"Your mother seems more social than your aunt. Does she have a lot of friends?"

"Yeah, she's real active and has lots of friends," I said. "She might look easy-going, but she can be tough as nails when she wants to. People don't con her easily. She knows what's happening."

"It sounds like you're proud of your mom, as you should be. I'm from Corvallis and have a couple of kids near your age and believe me, I'd also like to spend this kind of time with them. To really get to know how they're doing is probably best done by going off somewhere like this with them alone. You're fortunate to have a mother like you do."

"Thanks, Billy. Can I call you Billy?"

"Sure thing. Why don't you guys all come over after dinner for a beer?"

"Sounds good to me. See you later Billy."

# Sixteen: Twin

"HI THERE. IS IT HARRY?"

"That's right, and you're the man they call Twin?"

"Yes. My real name is Ken, but feel free to call me Twin. My friends all do."

"You seem to work more of the river than the others. And you're in deeper water. How come?" asked Harry from the bank.

"We all have our methods. Chief is the best fly-fisherman of us three. When he's had enough of one spot, he'll get out of the water and walk along the bank until he finds what looks like the next best spot and then he gets back in. I like to walk the entire river, provided it's not too deep to wade. I make a couple of casts, then take a couple of steps and that way I cover the whole area. I probably fish a lot of water unsuitable for trout, but the way I figure it, the fish have to swim through even the worst of it to get to where they're going. Chief, on the other hand, will not waste his time in places where he thinks the fish don't hang out. His way is more productive, but I love to walk in the river, that's half the fun for me. Fly-fishing is not as productive as the type of fishing you and your cousin are doing, but for me, it's the whole process that I find enjoyable. Sneaking up on the fish in their environment and presenting a fly that looks real to them. It's like a chess game I play with a real smart competitor on his home field."

The boy seemed interested, so as I talked, I kept up the fluid motion of my arm and pole.

"The fly at the end of your pole seems to be connected to, like an extension of, a thought about the fish," Harry called out to me.

"I couldn't have described it better myself." Nothing short of a neurological connection can explain the perfect swing of arm, pole, line, and fly as I drew the ever-increasing arc movement that culminated in a fly gracefully cutting through the air and landing gently right where I focused my gaze.

Harry's interest seems scientific, maybe microscopic. He seems to get what I am doing. He stood there on the bank, seemingly mesmerized as I continued my casts. No other human activity compares to the beauty of a man standing in moving water and gracefully presenting a fly to a wizened trout.

"I'm really impressed," Harry called out again. "I've

never seen fly-fishing up this close. My grandfather loved to fly-fish, but I never went with him. My mother says that when he was younger, it was all he ever wanted to do. Do you mind if I watch you for a while?"

"Better than that Harry, why don't we go over there to where there's a little more room on the bank behind you and I'll give you a lesson? Let you practice finessing the line. If it seems like something you'd enjoy, I can fix you up with a pole to practice with on your own. All three of us brought at least one extra and, believe it or not, we all got started by using someone else's rod."

I showed Harry how to hold the pole, how to swing his arm, how to feel the line. After ten minutes of experimenting with the cast, he laid the fly where he hoped it would land.

"If only my grandpa could see me now!" Harry beamed.

# Seventeen: Stacey

"MOM, I TRIED FLY-FISHING TODAY and I really like it," gushed Harry. "The guy named Twin showed me how and said he'd lend me his spare rod. It doesn't take any muscle; it's more of a finesse thing. Of course, the water is too cold to get in it without waders, so I was limited, but I sure had fun. I can definitely see what Grandpa liked about fly-fishing."

"Harry, that's great, but be careful. Borrowing rods and such. We don't really know those men. People have motives and we don't know theirs."

"Mom, you've got to quit distrusting everyone. Give Twin the benefit of the doubt."

"I'll give them the benefit of the doubt on some things," Cynthia said, "but when it comes to your safety, I'll reserve some distrust."

"Aunt Stacey can interact with strangers without letting her guard down. Watch how she can be friendly even if she's a little leery. She doesn't come off as defensive."

Overhearing Harry describe me like that felt good, but I need to make sure Cynthia doesn't take offense just because I'm more open with strangers.

"I think it's easier to get to know people when they are on vacation, away from home," I said to Harry. "People on trips, or at adjoining campsites, often want to share their experiences and sometimes their equipment, more so than neighbors back home. But you've got to realize that not all people are nice and it's good to have someone around like your mom to remind you. Keep in mind the value of the canary in the mineshaft—it's there to warn and protect all the others who are not paying attention. It's valuable for us to have a protective canary like your mother. God knows, I'm not the canary."

"I think that's a compliment," said Cynthia.

"It is, Mom. I know you watch over me, but don't take it to the point of worry. I'll be gone soon and I promise I'll be watchful. How could I not be vigilant after having been hatched by two canaries?"

&

At noon, with the sun at its full height, the forest seemed to pause and become silent. It was as if the animals, birds, and bugs were full after a morning of feeding and decided to all take a nap. The men at the other campsite had returned and I could hear them preparing their lunch.

Cynthia and I took out sandwich fixings to hold us over during our hike with the boys. I had thought they might want to do something alone, without us, but they said they were interested in exploring the area.

"Harry, why don't you ask your new friend over there if he knows of any good trails," suggested Cynthia, as she assembled the sandwiches.

"I'll go with you, Harry," said Cody. "Maybe we can bum a beer off of them."

"Cody! I did say you could have a maximum of two beers a day while we're up here," I said, "but remember that bumming a beer from a neighbor counts toward that."

"What will these two do when we're away at school?" Cody shouted in Harry's direction, making sure we could all hear as they walked towards the other campsite. "They'll have to find a hobby, or get a life!"

# Eighteen: Twin

"HI, WE HAVE A QUESTION," Harry said. "Do any of you know a trail we could hike this afternoon? One that's not too strenuous or the kind we could get lost on."

"There's several within an easy walk from camp. What do you guys think?" I asked Billy and Chief.

"How about the one that starts on the other side of the bridge?" asked Billy. "It's well marked and doesn't have forks to confuse you on the way back. When you get set to leave, come get me and I'll walk you to the beginning of the trail," said Billy.

I get it. Billy would be only too happy to provide guide service to such a fine looking woman as Stacey and her merry band. I noticed that he had already taken Cody under his wing back at the river this morning and I think he's planning on having another wing ready for Cody's mother. No harm in fantasy, I guess.

"Is there anything else we can do for you guys?" I

asked. The boys seemed undecided as to what to do next. As if they didn't know how to disengage from us and return to their mothers.

"Well," said Harry. "Cody was hoping you guys were drinking and that you'd share a beer with him. I guess that's how guys break the ice where he comes from."

"You're welcome to a cold one, Cody," offered Billy. "And I'll join you if you want. But we usually don't break out the booze until dinnertime."

"No problem, I can wait till then."

Male bonding occurs in many ways besides sharing a beer. I motioned for Harry to follow me over to my tent. "Wait here," I said, and went inside. When I emerged, I brought out a fly rod and handed it to Harry.

"You sure you don't mind?" Harry said.

"No problem. Try it next time you go to the river and see what you think. I have plenty of flies and I'll show you how to tie them to the tippet. You'll get the hang of it in no time. Doing it is the only way to find out if fly-fishing is for you."

"I'll sure take good care of your rod, Twin. I'd love to try it. Probably tomorrow."

"If that's the case, Harry, then tonight, before dark, we can get together to talk about flies—which ones to use and how to tie them on. Okay with you both? We'll even part with a couple of beers."

"That's more than okay," said Harry.

# Nineteen: Stacey

WHEN THE BOYS RETURNED, Harry seemed excited and Cody was annoyed, which made me wonder what was going on with my son. I'm well practiced at digging through the surface layer of Cody's façade and uncovering his emotions. Luckily, he makes my job easy because he wears them on his sleeve. After a bit of dancing around the issue, he spilled the beans.

It seems Harry is developing a friendship with the men more quickly than he is. Which is not what he expected to happen. And now he's jealous. After all, Harry is his non-adventurous cousin.

Cody said that Billy, the real cute neighbor, had been friendly with him this morning, but he couldn't imagine Billy lending him anything as precious as a fishing rod. He asked me if I thought there was more to Harry than we knew. I said there probably was.

"Okay, Mom. I feel better now. I'm still a little

annoyed, but by talking about it, I'm not as mad."

When we cleared away the lunch fixings, the four of us walked over to the men's camp. Their central, common area is much larger than ours is. And because the open space is wider, direct sunlight comes through and brings welcome afternoon warmth. Their campsite is also better organized. The fire pit is encircled by large, flat-topped rocks. In the center of the pit is one large rock, still hot, which held what appears to be a five-gallon pot of hot water—the kind I'd expect to see as the centerpiece at a downtown soup kitchen.

"What do you cook in that?" I asked.

Billy was quick to reply. "Hot water. We use it for bathing and for rinsing dishes. Whenever we take water out, we replenish it so that the next person has warm water too. We don't cook anything in that pot, but warm water when camping sure is nice. It's a real handy thing to have."

"Good thinking," I said. "We've been using a much smaller pot to boil water and we don't keep it going all day. It would be nice to have plenty of water to bathe because I'm not planning on going into the cold river for that." I smiled at Billy and feigned a shiver.

"Well, Stacey, anytime any of you want some warm water, just bring your pot over here, load up as much as you need and when you're done just go to the river and replace what you took. I'm sure none of us would mind," said Billy.

I noticed that the other men looked at him and smiled. Billy might be envisioning me bathing right here in his camp. Or maybe that's just me, always imagining where the male mind goes given half a chance.

"Are you guys ready to get going on your hike?" Billy asked, which changed the subject. But I doubt it altered his lecherous train of thought.

So, the two mothers, our two sons, and Billy set off on the short hike up the gravel road to a wooden bridge and the start of a trail. Billy relished his role as our guide. He pointed out and named the largest of the mountain peaks, some still topped with winter's snow. He suggested we use the mountain peaks to orient our sense of the direction. Fortunately, the peaks are so well defined, and so different from each other, that it should be easy to keep us heading the right way on the trail.

Billy also reminded us that our return would be downhill, with the river at the bottom. If we stayed on the trail, he guaranteed we could not possibly get lost.

"I know that 'Twin' is a nickname, but how did he get that name?" Harry asked.

"We gave him that name in the Marine Corps," Billy said. "He had an identical twin brother who was also assigned to our unit and we had a hell of a time telling them apart. Rather than try to figure out if we were talking to Kevin or to Ken, we called them both 'Twin.' They never called each other Twin, but everyone else did.

If you said, 'Hey, Twin,' they would both respond. Old habits are hard to change so Chief and I still call him Twin. I think he likes it because probably no one but us calls him that."

"Do the brothers still live near each other?" Harry asked.

"Oh, no. Kevin died less than a year after we returned from Iraq. In a car accident. It hit us all pretty hard. Ken and Kevin had been real close and shared so much of their lives. I think Twin likes the implication of that nickname. As if his brother is still here. Calling him Twin means we haven't forgotten Kevin."

"Well, I like him," said Harry. "And he told me to call him Twin. He's lending me a fly rod, and he taught me some moves this morning."

"That's what twins do," said Billy. "They share. Well, here's where I leave you."

We were standing on a dirt path that led through the tall trees toward the river. Looming in front of us was a sturdy, rough-hewn wooden bridge. It looks like it might have been built by big, sturdy men and would survive long after we are all long gone. It is a bridge built for foot traffic only, and spanned the river above a point of fast flow. The far side of the bridge marks the beginning of a trail that leads uphill to the jagged snow-topped mountain peaks. The trail appears to switch back upon itself for the climb.

"Billy would you mind taking our picture on the bridge?" I asked.

He almost tripped in his effort to respond as I handed him my smart phone. He seemed unconcerned that the others might find it odd he needed so much explanation from me on how the phone worked. Maybe no one else noticed. Damn, there I go again, assuming this man is interested in me. I can't seem to stop flirting, but Billy is so sweet.

To explain the photo controls, I had to lean my body into his, a position he made no attempt to alter. I enjoyed the nearness, and his rapt attention. He asked several questions that seemed to me like he was stalling, just getting in another minute or two of physical contact. Fortunately, he stepped away to get the photo of us before the teasing became uncomfortably apparent. With no further reason for Billy to linger, he finally left.

I was telling myself to nip this little amusement in the bud. I've been through this many times before and have always regretted not following my own advice. I've often allowed titillation to progress to the point where nipping things in the bud became hurtful to the silly male object of my insane amusement. I've never meant my amusements to deliberately hurt anyone, but sometimes that's how things turned out. Except possibly regarding my brother. Those amusements *were* intentionally hurtful.

I think my companions were happy Billy didn't ask to join us on our hike, but not me. I like the attractive man because he listened to my photo-taking instructions without implying he already knew it all. It was nice—for a change—to say something technical to a man without feeling bossy. So, yes, it's true—I have, accurately, been accused of being bossy, which generally culminates in an argument. But this man wanted my instruction and opinions and never adopted an attitude of superiority. And, bless his heart, he did say on parting that if he didn't see us back by five o'clock, he'd come searching.

&

From the start, Cody strode out front and set the pace. Again, he seems upset and apparently needs to relieve pent-up energy. Physical exertion will help settle his mind. It's what I do when I'm riled about something.

However, my son and I differ in how we handle the stuff that comes up. I tend to confront trouble head-on, while Cody looks for diversions to mask it and hopes whatever it is will go away in time. His ability to pause has its advantages and I wish I could do that, too. But it bothers me that he's walking by himself, deliberately not inviting Harry to join him, deliberately giving the impression he's angry. About what, I do not know.

I'm not going to confront him now because I have

too many other things on my mind. Hopefully, eventually, he'll work it out and join us again.

Conversation was my prime motive for this hike, but it seems all of us need silence for now to take in the visual and aromatic sensations of the forest. As the elevation and distance from the river increase, the density of the vegetation growing underneath the pines is thinning, which provides greater lines of sight. I feel better having a clearer idea of where we are in relation to this unfamiliar geography. The further we hike on this trail, the further we are from humans. We're delving deeper into a realm familiar only to the rest of the animal kingdom, and the further we go, the more abundant the evidence of animal life as their trails and droppings crisscross our path.

This trail meanders upward on a brown bed of fallen needles, cones, and deadfall, steadily rising uphill at a manageable angle. The trees are very tall; branches don't begin until thirty or forty feet up their thick trunks.

The climate is naturally dry in this area of the Northwest High Plateau, with most of the moisture falling during the months from Thanksgiving to Easter, and most often in the form of snow. The late summer sun filtering through in shafts gives the forest a mystical, godly feeling. The intense natural beauty, combined with the absence of other humans, fills me with awe.

After a bit of fear concerning our safety when we

first set out, now I just sigh. It seems at any moment a woodland fairy will appear—not a bear, bobcat, or wolf.

The scents are of moist earth and pine. Although the forest receives so little precipitation through summer and early fall, snowmelt from the mountaintops, moisture from the stream-fed river, and the cool shade of the enormous evergreens kept the forest floor cool and damp. I can smell the lovely moss and decay. This is truly a vibrant, healthy forest. I assume everyone in our quartet of hikers is just as consumed with the sensory wonders that surround us.

Harry is walking behind Cody and seems enthralled by this non-urban environment. I'm not sure he's noticed that Cody is avoiding him. Apparently, Harry developed a great interest in biology while in high school and, according to Cynthia, he placed Ecology high on his list of possible life pursuits. Perhaps this forest looks like a large, natural laboratory to him. Perhaps he feels the need to protect this ecosystem. I can think of no better calling for him.

Cynthia and I are keeping a comfortable pace walking together. The boys are never beyond our sight because, even though Cody is out front, he keeps glancing back and slows down whenever we lag.

Cody, the explorer, seeks whatever lies ahead. Success for him is based on how far we go and the amazing things we see along the way. I bet Harry would rate the trip based on the varieties of life he can identify. I base our success on how well the group enjoys the day.

"This trip has been a nice surprise," said Cynthia. "I had a picture of other campsites in my mind and when we first got here, I was a bit worried. This area is much more desolate than anywhere I've ever been. I had visualized pulling into a campground that looks like a little neighborhood of people—with running water, women's restrooms, and a camp host who provides written rules. But here, we're alone with only a camp table and then, a half hour later, we're joined by strangers who pitch their tents right in our shadow. Thank God for you because I'd have packed up and driven back home right then. Now, I'm glad we stayed. The men seem reasonable and cultured and the boys fit in great with them. I'm glad one of them is teaching Harry about fly-fishing. I watched Harry light up. His father is too busy to do that sort of thing and I have no experience."

"Even if you did have the experience, Cynthia," I said, "those kinds of lessons are best passed on by an older guy, not us. I noticed the joy in Harry's voice when he talked about that guy called Twin. Some story, wasn't it, about the death of his brother after the war? Being a twin teaches the importance of give and take behavior and he probably misses his brother horribly much. Maybe befriending Harry is nice for him too. And I'm really impressed with Harry's way with those men. He seems so confident, yet humble."

"Nice of you to say, Stacey. Harry's life has been tough because Loren has such difficulty getting close to anyone. Loren is so uptight, but I don't know how to ease his tension. I don't like it and I've never felt so distant from him before. We talk about family business, but never about anything going on inside. He finds fault with everything I suggest and sometimes I get scared for my physical safety. Although he has never hit me, it seems inevitable that someday he might. Probably because I'm less inclined to take his shit anymore. Pardon my language."

That last statement made me laugh out loud. "You never have to apologize to me for language, Cynthia," I said. "I could probably make those men in the next campsite blush. Growing up, Loren had anger issues, but never did anything physical. He's never been a fighter, but he was emotionally vicious. And I appreciate what you said about being less scared with Cody and I being here with you, but I admit I was nervous, too. We haven't even heard another car since we got here. We really are isolated, more than I thought we'd be, and so we need to remain friendly to those guys, but not too friendly. They are probably fine, but you never know."

"The boys linked us to them, but we don't want to erase our boundaries—even if the boys have," agreed Cynthia.

"Loren is another matter entirely. What you said about my brother, although hard to hear, doesn't surprise me. I always thought he was a woman hater, except for you of course, but maybe he just devalues everyone."

"Loren is sarcastic of everyone, even his few friends, but he has increasingly drawn himself inward. He doesn't listen to anyone, and I don't think that's good for him or us. He's drinking more and that's why I feel more afraid of him. He reaches a point when he's drinking where he can't seem to control himself. I dread what it will be like at home when Harry leaves. Although Loren seems oblivious of Harry, I think the presence of his son holds him in check about how far to go with his anger. It seems I am no longer a deterrent."

I put an arm around Cynthia in a gesture of support. I'd hoped this trek through the forest would evoke close sharing, but I hadn't intended it to get this emotional.

"I'll always stand with you and Harry if it comes to that," I said. "Just know that I pray for Loren and until he comes around, I'm with you. Let's look for a spot to rest and snack on the apples and nuts I stashed in my daypack."

When we stopped and sat on a deadfall log, the boys backtracked as if on cue. Harry told us about the delicate ecological processes he'd been observing even though his explanation was beyond my ability to understand. Just watching him share his interest was joy enough for me.

"We're beyond the sound of the river," Cody announced. "Deep into the Eagle Cap Wilderness." He pointed out how much closer the mountain peaks were, and how, if we stayed on the trail, we couldn't get lost. Harry was absorbed with the microenvironment, Cody with the macro.

"Are you trying to say we should start heading back to camp?" asked Cynthia.

"Not at all," answered Cody. "I think we should go another hour and then head back. It'll be much faster going downhill."

After a rest, we proceeded with Cody again in the lead, but the rest of us in a closer line.

"I guess I've gotten so accustomed to living with a man who never expresses his desires," Cynthia said, "that I've gotten to a point where I look for hidden meaning in all male statements. I thought Cody was saying we should turn around."

I didn't respond to Cynthia's statement and we just walked silently for a while.

"You're doing a great job leading us," I called ahead to my son. "What do you think of this area? We probably have all we need here—a little snow, mountains, forest, river, and maybe even wild animals."

He didn't reply.

"Cody is my wilderness man. I always feel safe with him around," I said loud enough for everyone to hear. I hoped my statement would help him out of his funk, if it still persisted.

A moment later, Cody halted, spun around, and signaled for us to get down and be quiet. He pointed to a hill that paralleled our trail. We all strained to see what had grabbed Cody's attention and caused him to adopt a position of danger readiness. Harry gestured across the draw separating us from the hill, a football field distance away.

I was the last to see it. Through the trees, I finally detected a large, adult brown bear standing on all fours, definitely looking directly at us.

With a finger to his lips and eye contact with us all, Cody conveyed a silent command. If this bear chose to charge, he would be upon us in less than a minute and we had foolishly come unprepared. We'd taken no weapons with us. But Cody had a plan for this harrowing situation. He scoured the ground until he found two rocks the size of baseballs.

My first thought was—how much good will those rocks be against a charging bear? But then I saw Cody, still crouching, holding the rocks one in each hand, begin to bang them together, which made a loud clacking noise. He continued striking the rocks until the bear slowly turned and moved on.

We watched until the bear disappeared over the ridgeline and then all of us, without any consultation, backtracked down the trail. Harry took the lead and Cody remained on guard in the rear. We walked in silence for a while before anyone felt safe enough to talk. And then all we talked about was the bear.

From that point on, we became a team. Maybe encountering the bear helped us all to move physically closer, like a herd of animals in an environment rife with predators. You know—safety in numbers. Or maybe the fright exposed our vulnerabilities and instinctively we knew that only through teamwork would we endure.

Cody signaled that the danger was over when he again took the lead and set a steady pace downhill. Although that particular bear might be gone, I figured it was not the only bear in this wilderness, so I remained vigilant for the rest of our hike. I also noticed that Cody continued to carry his two rocks all the way to the bridge that crossed our river.

I was proud of my son for the coolness he showed when confronted with danger. I believe it's best to avoid all bears not in a cage. On the hike downhill, we wondered if it was a black or brown bear, and if we'd had a life-threatening event. It all seemed to happen so fast. We impressed ourselves because none of us had panicked. We all agreed that Cody had been courageous and wise. He'd used a technique his father, the coach, had taught him. I'm quite sure Cody can hardly wait to tell his dad.

"I know I'll never forget this adventure. I'll always have this time in the forest to look back on," said Cynthia.

I noticed my breathing finally returned to normal.

&

"Harry," I said, "would you take this pot over there when you go for your fly-tying lesson with Twin? Some hot water would help because I'm pretty ripe after that hike."

"I'll go with you, Harry," said Cody "and, Mom, it's not tying flies that he's teaching. Twin's flies are probably store-bought. He'll be showing us how to tie the flies to the line and I'll probably need to interpret for Harry later on."

Harry flashed Cody his middle finger, which I witnessed. I smiled at Harry and gave him a thumbs-up.

# Twenty: Twin

"HEY, TWIN, IS THIS A GOOD TIME to bug you about tying flies on the line?" asked Harry.

"Interesting choice words, Harry," said his cousin loud enough so all could hear.

"Good as any," I replied. "Let's move to the table where we can stretch out the pole and line. We always keep a portion of the table clear so we can do just this sort of thing. There are four lines on this reel, each tied one behind the other. It is very important that the knots tying them together are strong enough to not come undone, yet small enough to pass freely through the rod. You don't want to hook a large fish only to lose him because a knot opened. Worse than that, you don't want the guilt of knowing you've left a fish swimming around in the river with a hook in his mouth trailing line. We rarely keep any fish we catch, so we want to do all we can to minimize their experience. We want to catch and release them with as little stress as possible."

"Will I need to learn several kinds of knots?" asked Harry.

"Not yet, unless you become addicted," I answered. "Closest to the spool on the reel is the backing line. You'll probably never see it unless you catch something big that takes off on you for a long swim. That backing is tied to the fly line, which is colored and weighted. That's what provides the weight needed to sling out on your cast. Fly-fishing doesn't take strength as much as it does finesse. The finesse of slinging the weighted line out takes practice, but you showed a good hang of that this morning."

The boys were all eyes and ears, attentive. I figure they will be in good shape if they carry this same level of attention into their college classes.

"Next, I attach about five feet of 'leader' to the fly line," I said. "The leader is a filament that comes in a variety of strengths depending on what size and type of fish you are after. This is the setup for trout up to maybe twenty inches long. Attached to the leader is an even thinner line called the tippet, which is intended to be so thin that the fish can't see it. But thick enough to hold the fly. Since we fly fisherman are constantly changing flies because we always believe the next type of fly will be what the fish want, the tippet gets shortened each time we cut off a fly and tie on a new one. New tippets will be needed often, but you won't have to worry about that today. You have four or five feet of it already on there, which is plenty. I use a different knot for tying line than I do for tying on flies. I know four types of knots and that gets me through all situations."

"Why don't you use the strongest size leader and tippet for all your fishing," asked Cody. "Just in case you hook something big and strong like a steelhead?"

"Good question, because that goes to what I consider the fun of fly-fishing. I always use the lightest setup that will get the job done. The light rod and line provides the most excitement when you get a strike. As a fisherman, you call on all your skills and finesse so as not to lose him. And because it's a better sport with light gear. Sure, you might lose some fish if they're big, but you'll also hook more because the lighter leader and tippet is almost invisible. When I'm fishing for steelhead or salmon, I go to a heavier rod and line. We all bring more than one rod and reel, setups for different types of fish. That's why I have an extra one you can borrow. The one you'll use is set up for brook trout and bull trout."

Then I demonstrated how to tie a simple cinch knot for changing flies.

"Harry," I said, "I'll be giving you a variety of flies, all with barbless hooks. I want to make sure you can easily remove any fish you catch. The easier the release, the better it is for the fish, and the better the karma for the fisherman. I don't care if you keep the trout you catch, but you will eat any fish you take. If you both want to fish with flies at the same time, I'll ask Chief or Billy to lend you another rod."

"Naw, don't worry about that," Cody said. "We can trade off tomorrow, one of us with flies, and one with gear."

I smiled. So, Cody is familiar with the term that fly-fishermen use when referring to those who use spinning rods with lures—gear fishermen.

Harry picked up the rod for a fun trial run tomorrow, but before leaving, they filled both a pot with hot water and some plastic jugs with filtered drinking water. Cody said he would be right back with river water to replace it.

"Why don't you guys come back after supper with your moms and join us for a beer around the fire?" Billy called out. "You can bring the water back then."

# Twenty-One: Stacey

THE TWO BOYS EXCITEDLY TOLD CYNTHIA and me that we'd been invited to join the men that evening at their campsite. We weren't as enthused. I'd planned on having a close mom-son conversation around the campfire that evening, and every evening for the rest of the week. I don't really want to share him with strangers.

Then I realized my annoyance probably stems from the change in expectations. I can see Cody is looking forward to talking more with the men. So, that means my ability to garner the attention of men obviously doesn't work with regard to my son. Jealousy is not an emotion I am acquainted with, so it's interesting that I'm jealous about my son's focus of attention. Which makes me contemplate the fact that someday he'll find a life partner and I'll be relegated to the obsolete category. Being replaced by a stranger is a frightening new thought for me. Yow! My firstborn is already blazing a path away from me and I need to adjust.

Okay. I know I've nurtured and prepared him well. I am capable of following him into his future. My role now is to share him and revel in his journey.

Cynthia's mouth is taut, creating a grim expression. And her voice has a hesitancy to it. She's reluctant to agree to the camp intermingle. She's not comfortable around strangers, especially those of the opposite sex. Especially male strangers drinking alcohol. She has almost no experience drinking in bars, and I suspect her husband and her church have warned her repeatedly about the dangers in mixing alcohol and strangers. I can hear Loren now—strangers have hidden passions, men are interested only in sex and self-pleasure, strange men will hurt you. Cynthia's only recourse is to trust her son, and to pray.

"So these two young men will be going off soon to the same college. How exciting," said Billy when we gathered around the men's campfire. "I hope you guys take better advantage of your education than I did. When I came home from overseas, I used the G.I. Bill to pay for four years of partying at Oregon State University. I thought I owed it to myself to make up for some lost years spent in the Marine Corps. Although, in all that partying, I did find a wife and we've been together, living in the shadow of that school ever since."

"I'm not paying for my son to find a wife," I said, laughing. "But I appreciate what you're saying about the importance of schoolwork over having fun. I have faith these guys are a more serious pair than I was. At least, I hope so."

"Glad you have faith in me 'cause I thought I'd spend the first couple of years there just chilling until I find a girl to do my work for me."

"That's it, go to your tent right now!" I admonished, feigning annoyance.

"Let him at least finish his beer," Billy said playfully.

Cynthia obviously didn't get the humor because she gave me a squinted-eye look and tightened her lips. She'd missed the sarcasm.

Harry broke the ice by laughing and giving his mother a loving hug. "And that's the reason I'll be Cody's roommate. I'm being sent to make sure he does something more in college than just chill."

"I'm glad to hear that," said Billy. "Neither of you want to go to school for four years and come out a car salesman like me. Get a good degree like Chief did. Turn it into a meaningful career."

"There's nothing wrong with what Billy does," said the mostly silent Chief. "Billy is so good at sales that he makes a lot more money than Twin and I do. I think a college degree made a difference for him as it does for anyone, no matter what they do. You boys are lucky to have family so supportive. You don't want to miss out on this opportunity."

"Is it okay to call you Chief? I think you're a Native American and I don't want to be disrespectful," said Harry, who seemed to be loosening up after one beer.

"It's no disrespect and for sure—call me Chief. It's a name I picked up in the Marine Corps, and at first the name bothered me, but then I realized, to those guys it indicated an element of respect. In that branch of service, they call all Native American Indian men 'Chief' and they assumed we were all better than the rest in hunting and tracking skills. Granted, that stereotypes us, but it was a bias of respect and admiration. Those skills are prized in the infantry, as they still are in my culture. Because of that, I appreciate the nickname. Very few people call me Chief outside of these two, and a few other vets I keep in touch with, so I like the name. It bonds us as friends. Call me Chief, or Ben. I'll answer to both. But not to Mr. Troxler."

"With respect, then, Chief, I'd really like to talk to you sometime about what you do for a living because that's very much what I might be studying in college," said Harry. "I plan to major in Biology and especially Ecology and that sort of thing."

"Anytime, Harry," said Chief. "Most people have the

wrong impression of what I do and think of me as a wilderness cop. I'm far from that but I do have little patience for people who defile the land and especially for those who make a living raping it. I'll be happy to explain my job to you anytime."

Apparently, right now is not that time because Chief rose and excused himself. I took his return to his tent as a hint that it was time for us all to retire. By then, the boys had finished their two beers apiece and seemed to fit in well with the men. I enjoyed the attention I got from Billy, and held my own with all that male-dominated talk by using sarcasm and jibes. Cynthia hadn't said much all evening, but she paid close attention and seemed somewhat comforted by how easy the time had been.

While walking back to our campsite, flashlight directing the way, I commented to Cynthia that I had never seen my son drink alcohol with adults other than family members. Cynthia said she was happy to see how well Harry fit in.

"I guess it's all part of letting go," Cynthia said.

# Twenty-Two: Twin

"YOU CAN STICK YOUR TONGUE back in your mouth now, Billy, and quit drooling," I said. "When Stacey is around, you're the guy you were twenty years ago. Just don't forget the family in Corvallis."

"Relax, Twin, I'm just playing around. I'd never let things get out of hand. Thinking about it and doing it are two different things. My thinker hasn't stopped working and I don't think yours has either. Don't tell me you don't fantasize when you see someone with a nice butt and so attractive."

"But I'm careful not to play it too far," I said. "I might not be able to reverse gears exactly when I want."

"Taking chances is what makes life interesting and I think it keeps a guy young. Anyway, nothing is gonna come of it out here with you guys and her family as chaperones. We're just developing a friendship, is all."

"Well, Billy, she looks like the kind of woman that

would chew you up and spit you out with no second thoughts. The kind where if you flirted with her too much, she just might take you up on it and not release you until she's had enough. You might find you're out of your league when it comes to playing games with her. Just saying," I said.

"Gimme a break, Twin. You make it sound like I've got no will power and no ability to make decisions. Nobody's the boss of me. She can't control me—even if she is one hot mama."

"We'll see. By the way, I'm not the only person paying attention to the vibes between you two. Her son, Cody, clammed up when he noticed you were focusing your attention on his mother. You and he were the first to introduce yourselves and become friends. Now, you're more interested in his mother. It's not good to make a kid jealous that way."

"That's the first good point you've made," said Billy. "I'll watch for that. You know I don't want to screw up any family relationships. I was just enjoying making new friends."

I rose from my camp chair and swatted my friend on the back of his head, which caused his cap to land in the fire. I headed to my tent.

"Asshole," was the last word I heard from Billy as he jumped up to retrieve his hat.

# Twenty-Three: Cody

"DO YOU REALLY THINK WE SHOULD stay out here much longer?" I asked. "When we're not being watched by bears, it's starting to get boring. A guy can do only so much fishing and hiking with his mother. I kind of miss my friends back in McCall." I knew I was complaining, but Harry was annoying me. We were just a couple of feet apart in our sleeping bags.

"I'm excited to try fly-fishing tomorrow and if I like it, I can see doing quite a bit more while I'm here," Harry replied. "That is, if those guys will loan me their stuff. The other thing is I'd like to talk to Chief about the work he does and get advice for college courses. I'm thinking that I'd like more time here than just the week we planned."

"Well, you sure did find some folks that fit right into your plans. And truly, I'm happy for you," I said and really meant it. "I'll shut up about wanting to go home, but don't go expecting that I'm gonna do all the things that you want to do at school."

"Of course I know that you'll make your own friends and have your own interests. I'm a loner. I take pleasure in solitary time, so I don't see any problem there. Maybe that's why fly-fishing is so interesting to me. It's a solitary thing. I really enjoy being out in nature like we have here. Maybe this is more my kind of lifestyle, living in a forest, away from crowds, apart from man-made stress. This is the best place I've ever been. I know I can't stay forever, but I sure would like to max it out."

"It's great that you're having fun here Harry, but when we get to the university, I plan to not be solitary."

"No problem, Cody. I won't get in your way. You'll see—I'll be really easy to get along with as a roommate."

"Yep, we'll see," I replied. I have no idea why I'm so grumpy.

# Twenty-Four: Stacey

"THE BOYS HAVE STOPPED TALKING," said Cynthia.

"Don't let me forget to ask them to bring us lots of hot water from that other camp," I said. "I want to give myself a good wash tomorrow morning before they go off fishing. I miss having a bathtub."

"I hope that your interest in sprucing up has nothing to do with Billy," Cynthia cautioned.

"Are you kidding?" I said. "I'm not out here to impress anyone. And I'm not interested in some married car salesman who hasn't bathed. No, I just don't like to smell like this."

"If you dab on some perfume, Stacey, does that mean I should worry?"

"That's right, Cynthia. But I'll let you know when to worry. It's okay that I sometimes flirt with guys I think are nice, and I think those three next door are nice. But, believe me, I can handle myself around men."

"Of course you can," Cynthia said. "I've been watching you. You're so much better at that than I am. The truth is, sometimes I'm attracted to a man, but whenever that happens, I run the other way. I just clam up and don't talk at all. For instance, that guy, Chief. The way he spoke to my son stirred me. He will probably give Harry more advice and encouragement in one day than Loren does in a year, and I appreciate that. And I find him attractive. I was impressed with his wisdom and self-assuredness. He offered his opinion only when asked and even then, he didn't mince words. Immediately, I forced myself to back off from him. I think it would be too dangerous for me to get to know him any better. I can't trust myself like you do, Stacey. You have skills around men, but I don't, so forgive me if I implied you were as weak as me."

"That's nice of you to say, but Cynthia, what you consider weakness, I think of as strength," I said. "And I am happy that you care enough to be concerned for me. But I have no interest in Billy beyond his friendship with Cody and the fact that they are our neighbors for a week in a place where it pays to have friendly neighbors. "

"Yeah, you're right, Stacey. Okay. I'll force myself to lighten up. I'd like to join you for a morning bath. We could have the boys fill every pot with hot water once those guys take off fishing for the morning. We'll have plenty of time to replace it so they won't even notice when they get back."

"It will be like a spa in nature. Lack of bathing facilities has got to be the biggest disadvantage of remote camping, but those guys are making it easy on us. See why it's so important to flirt with those silly men?" I said with a wink and a nefarious giggle. "Okay, sister-in-law, time for some shut-eye."

My body is tired from the hike, but my mind is surprisingly energized. Lying here, stretched out in my sleeping bag, is the first chance I've had to sort through the day. I wonder if those guys in their tents have to take inventory every night before they doze off.

I wonder what Cynthia thinks now that she's seen how easy it is for her son to bond with non-related adult males. He's not afraid to ask questions, and has the capacity to listen attentively to what they say. He's like an eaglet being fed the regurgitated food from the mouth of another bird. It's no mystery to me that he's such a good student.

Harry displays a humility he obviously didn't inherit from his father. I wonder where Harry learned such an endearing trait.

Humility will probably come slower to Cody. Lord knows his father doesn't have any. I'm thankful that teamwork and friends have always been important to him. He likes having things his way, but Cody can adjust when he has to. I'm so proud of the way he reacted to the bear today. He was brave, decisive, and I sure like the way he never hesitated. He just took control. We needed him and he responded. Best yet, he didn't brag or even talk about it much afterwards. He has confidence in most stereotypical male exploits.

Ah. Male exploits. That Billy guy sure is interesting. I bet he and I would have hit it off even if we'd met somewhere else. He's handsome, appears healthy, and can listen. What can I say? The allure of the chase is still enticing for me. I like the energy. Playful sexuality has always enlivened me and I guess I should be grateful that I haven't lost that. Fortunately, the energy that increases my heartbeat and heightens my senses rarely causes trouble. If there was trouble, it wouldn't fall on me—just the shoulders of the men who take my interest too seriously. So? They might feel rejected, but that's not my concern. Like with the bear today, I enjoy being stirred up—but only at a distance, and with enough room to allow my retreat when I've had enough.

Lately, thankfully, the allure of what is forbidden has diminished for me. Perhaps I don't need that drama because I'm getting older. I don't want to think about that now.

My intentions with new friends are honorable. I'm just adding a bit of spice to brief interplay with our camping neighbors. Soon they will be out of sight and out of mind.

Here I am, a forty-year-old, contently married woman on a camping trip with her oldest son for the purpose of getting in some quality time with him. I must keep that goal in mind. I must avoid all other interests.

I must get some sleep.

&

It's cold this morning! I'd guess it to be in the mid-forties, which means it won't be warm enough to bathe until mid-day. Cynthia and I have plenty of time to prepare, which begins with finding a suitable private location.

We agreed to approach our bathing in two stages. First, we will attend to our hair. A quick river wash and slow warm water rinse will be followed by a resupply of hot water for a repeat of stage one, but for our bodies.

"Let's head to the river bank to find a place that has privacy and easy access," I suggested.

We found a flat rock that will serve as a good launching platform for a quick entry into waist-deep water. The rock juts out into a pool at a bend in the river, so the water slows there.

"Do you realize how cold that water is? We could get brain freeze," worried Cynthia, still not completely sold on this idea.

"Our brains won't freeze, but it might feel like it,

Cynthia," I said. "Anyway, let's try the water; it might not be as bad as you think. If we can pull this off once, then we'll be able to do it again in a couple of days."

"It's not like we have to look good for anyone," Cynthia said. "But you're right. I know I'll feel better afterwards, so okay, I'm in. Two pots of warm water apiece should be enough. But, Stacey, I would never do this if you weren't here."

"We should wash our hair first because that will take the most water. Two round trips to the well should take no more than twenty minutes if we stick to our plan and don't dawdle. And no one will be the wiser."

We decided to let the boys head off for their fishing after breakfast and we'd fetch the warm water ourselves. That way, the water wouldn't cool down as we waited for the sun to warm the air.

By late morning, I figured the day was as warm as it was going to get. "Let's head out to the deserted men's camp," I suggested.

"I feel like a soldier behind enemy lines," Cynthia whispered.

With our giddy hearts beating rapidly, we silently filled four pots with hot water from the big cauldron on the men's dying fire and stole away leaving no trace of our presence.

We dashed off, giggling like schoolgirls making off with a prize from the boy's locker room.

The sun was direct at the river's edge and had warmed the flat rock we'd selected. I decided Cynthia would be the first to lie down and dip her head into the water. I told her to bring her head back up quickly, and I would add the shampoo to suds it up.

"Come on, you chicken. People all around the world do this on a regular basis. Make Harry proud of you," I urged my sister-in-law.

"I've changed my mind. Stacey, you go first. After all, this was all your idea." I'd never heard Cynthia so determined.

"Okay, but make sure you're right there with the two pots of rinse water. Give me the shampoo and say a prayer for me. I know you're good at that."

I stretched out on the rock on my stomach and let my hair drop into the water. Maybe for the same reason that haircuts don't hurt, I felt no pain. However, once I immersed my entire scalp to get the roots thoroughly wet, I felt the burning cold on the back of my neck and ears.

I pulled my head up, quickly soaped my scalp, and urged Cynthia to pour the warm rinse on my head. At home, I always used hair conditioner, but under the circumstances, I was willing to forgo that step. It dawned on me why far less conditioner is sold in third world countries than shampoo. Not all bathing is as pleasurable as the warm showers I take back home.

When Cynthia poured the second pot of warm rinse water over my head I said, "That's better than sex. Or at least better than sex with most men. Now it's your turn."

"Shiiiit!" screeched Cynthia, after her head rose from under the water. "Are you kidding! I can't do this!"

"Come on, get your whole head in there," I told her.

"Just hold my damn ankles like I asked you! God, I don't want to fall into this shitty river," screeched Cynthia.

I would never have suspected her capable of using such colorful language. Laughing, I said, "And you might want to wash your mouth out when you're down there!"

I was glad we chose to wash our hair first, as that was a lot worse than washing our bodies. We wrapped our heads with towels and snuck back to get more warm water. Again, it felt as if we were invading sacred male ground. We didn't know if any of the men had returned to their camp.

But we were even more brave for the second excursion. We filled our four pots with more hot water, then lingered in enemy territory long enough to scout around. We checked out their food stash, and how each man arranged his personal space. This was far more adventurous than back-home bathing.

Washing our bodies proved less exciting than washing our hair. One of us watched for intruders while the other undressed and use a cloth dipped in warm water to wash. Then we made sure to replace all the water we'd taken. We added a bit more fire under the cauldron.

Cynthia and I ran back to our campsite holding hands, carrying the empty pots with our other. We laughed and luxuriated in our adventure well planned.

"That's it for me," Cynthia said once we settled down. "One bath a week will do me fine."

"I didn't realize how cold that water would be," I said. "I love being clean, but there are limits and I think I've reached mine."

# Twenty-Five: Cody

"LET'S FIND A PLACE WHERE THERE'S PLENTY OF ROOM for our back cast. I don't want to tell Twin we lost all his flies in the branches of trees," said Harry.

"Maybe upriver, in the direction Chief goes," I said. "It's too cold to get in the water without waders, but maybe we can find a spot where the trees are not right up to the edge."

Fifteen minutes later, we found a place where the water was deeper and a couple of large rocks were exposed allowing a fisherman, if careful, to reach farther into the river without getting wet. Harry and I agreed the spot would be safe for the over-head practice and backward casting of fly-fishing.

"I wish we'd thought to bring waders from home," I said.

"Why don't you try the fly rod first," offered Harry.

Smart kid, I figured. He knew I'd lose interest if I

were relegated to just an observer role.

"If you want," Harry said, "I can explain the tips that Twin showed me yesterday."

"Don't bother, I'll be fine," I replied. "Why don't you find a place to fish using my pole, and I'll come trade with you in a while?"

"You're not pissed off at me are you, Cody?"

"No. But, Harry, sometimes you do bother me. I wouldn't call it getting pissed off. Sometimes you seem smug and elite. This whole bit with the fly-fishing and ecology stuff is annoying," I said, since he asked.

"Are you sure you want to share a dorm room with me? I know that was decided by our parents, but I've never asked you straight out."

"You're right. It was a plan cooked up by our parents because it sounded logical to them. I just need to know you better. I realize you don't mean me any disrespect but, Harry, sometimes your attitude just seems off."

"Our interests are different, and that's okay with me. Will *you* be able to handle it?" asked Harry.

"Actually, I think your interests are great," I admitted. "I wish I were interested in them, too. Maybe that's what annoys me about you. You just seem to have everything so together."

"I just want you to always be up front with me, Cody. If I bug you too much, let me know and I can change, or we'll change, or we'll get different roommates.

It's no big deal, Okay?"

"I've watched lots of fishermen in and around McCall," I said. "If I need help, I'll ask Billy, or one of the other guys, not you. No offense, but some people know more than you do. You're my cousin, but Harry, there's some things you don't know. I'll come and find you when I'm ready to trade back and use my rod."

I've watched many fly fishermen in the favorite fishing spots back in McCall. And I would rather figure out the techniques for myself rather than have this smug bookworm cousin from the city tell me what he himself learned only yesterday in fifteen minutes with Twin. It was good to finally tell that know-it-all cousin of mine how I feel about him. I feel better now. More like myself.

I'm slinging the fly around and luckily haven't tangled the line in vegetation although I've spent considerable time unsnarling tangled line. I haven't caught any trout either. I know it's hasn't even been an hour, but I'm done with fly-fishing and want my spinning rod back. Everyone knows the more time the fly, lure, or bait spends in the water, the better your chances of catching fish.

"How'd you do?" Harry asked when I returned.

"Not too bad," I lied. "I had a couple on, but they shook themselves off before I could land them. It was fun, but I'm kind of used to my rod, so I think I'll stick to that. I'll trade places with you now."

Later, back in camp, Harry told our moms that productivity would come in time if he just developed the proper techniques. He went on and on, describing the grace and full body sensation of each cast and presentation of the fly onto the surface of the water.

"Fly-fishing requires patience," Harry said, "but no real strength. It's a communion of body and rod that unfolds from a spot inside me and extends to the fly at the other end. With each cast, I feel my entire being involved, as if the rod is an extension of my mind. If I remain coordinated, almost dance-like, I can initiate the cast and observe the delicate fly land on the surface of the water. It's as if the pole and I are one entity that moves through air and water. I love this, Mom," Harry said. "My goal is to present the artificial fly so that it mimics a fly in nature. For sure, Mom! This is such a thrill!"

Blah, blah, blah, is what I heard.

# Twenty-Six: Stacey

CYNTHIA AND I PREPARED SANDWICHES for Cody and Harry, but they returned long enough only to grab one and a can of soda, then headed out again. They left behind their heavier clothing because the direct sun was strong on the river. Neither of them mentioned how clean we looked.

Cody was nonstop bragging about all the fish he'd caught, and Harry was excited about his experiments with fly-fishing. Neither were interested in hanging around with us at the campsite.

I heard the men across the way straggle back for their lunch and afternoon siestas. I would have been happy to walk over for a visit, but I knew Cynthia would be reluctant, so I kept that idea to myself. After all, those men aren't here to socialize with strangers. Running into them while strolling the path along the river is one thing, barging into their camp uninvited is another.

Figuring that Cynthia would settle in reading a book, I decided to hike along the river. I couldn't get lost and it would afford me an opportunity to get out of camp and see what captures the attention of all these men.

&

"Where's Harry?" I asked when I saw Cody casting from the bank.

"He's further up-river somewhere. If you're worrying about him, Mom, he can't get lost. A bear might fight him for a fish, but there's no way he could get lost."

"Stop that. If your Aunt Cynthia heard you talk like that, she might pack up and return to Boise."

"Maybe that wouldn't be so bad. Harry can be a butthead. That's why I'm glad he's out of sight sometimes. I'm beginning to wonder if it was such a good idea for us to room together at the university."

"Don't start that, Cody," I said. "You leave for school in two weeks and the plans have all been made. Give it one year with Harry. If you want to change, I'll listen then. You're used to being the oldest child at home, but soon you'll be living in a dormitory full of guys just like you and you won't be able to boss them around. You'll get along best if you don't always demand your way. Sometimes, I think you have too much of me in you." I was trying to be serious, but I couldn't help but giggle.

"Sometimes I think of Harry like he's a younger brother who I need to teach and protect. And he can be obnoxious, just like a little brother."

"Cody, you and Harry have different strengths and I'm hoping you'll both realize that during this next year. So, tell me. Where are all the rest of the fishermen?"

"They're all further up-river. Are you planning to go scare away their fish too?"

"Actually, Cody, maybe you're more like your father."

"Just remember my father when you're talking to them. Sometimes you seem more like a sister than my mom around men, and well, it feels weird to me."

"I can handle myself, don't worry. You're growing up, but I'm still your mom. I won't embarrass you."

&

"Hello, Twin," I called out so as not to scare the man waist deep in the water. "Are you doing good? Isn't that what you guys usually say?"

"Oh, hi, Stacey. I'm not catching nearly as many as I'd like, but it's all good." Twin began walking towards me.

"I don't mean for you to stop what you're doing. Cody tells me I scare the fish when I barge in on him. I think it's just an excuse to get rid of me. He tells me how many fish he catches, but I never see him doing it."

"Well, I've seen him catch some. I move up and down the river more than the others do, and I've seen Cody when he didn't know I was watching. He seems to be a real outdoorsman."

"He gets that from his dad and the fact that we live in a part of Idaho well-suited for outdoor activities," I said.

"I thought all of Idaho was well-suited for outdoor activities," said Twin. "At least that's been the case everywhere I've gone in that state."

Twin began casting again just off the bank.

"I live on the Central Coast of Oregon and it sure is beautiful there, but my wife and stepchildren are rooted to our business and the community. I don't get much time to get out and do this sort of thing."

I sat down on the bank and asked him about his bed and breakfast. He said everyone in the family is involved in running the business. Everyone has their own role in making it a success.

Part of me is envious. My family all have varied interests and we rarely share in each other's successes or failures. It must make a family stronger when they participate in such important common interests. It's hard for me to imagine the members of my family rallying around any one specific project.

Twin said this was his second marriage. I wonder if

it's working out better for him. Other people's relationships interest me and Twin has no hesitancy in talking about his. He's very proud of what his wife and stepdaughters have accomplished.

After half an hour sharing our histories and styles of living, I can picture Twin in his coastal home. I'm good at listening and hearing between the lines and filling in what wasn't said. Twin is a man who appreciates what he has.

"After twenty years of being with my husband," I said, "I think I'm finally figuring out what I need in a marriage. I've been fortunate, but most of what I thought I needed is just not that big a deal. My husband is trusting and doesn't rely too much on me for his happiness. In fact, your family and mine seem a lot alike. I've always admired people who can blend into an already-made family. I don't know that I could do that, but it sounds like you've done well." I meant that as a compliment.

Twin was silent for a while. He seemed deep in thought. I hoped I hadn't offended him.

"My husband and I have a real good life together, but we enjoy our time apart. Coach is so supportive of me taking this time with Cody. I get the feeling that you have the same sort of arrangement with your wife."

Twin began wading up-river.

"I do," he called back.

&

"Hi, there, Billy! I've been walking this path checking in on everybody. I feel like an assembly line supervisor. Do you need any help?" I asked sarcastically.

"Help from you, sure," replied Billy with a big smile. "The worst part of this type of fishing is trying to walk a rocky riverbed without falling. Sometimes I want to get somewhere fast and that's when I inevitably fall. I'd hate to do that trying to get closer to you."

Watching him slowly approach gave me time to reflect on how this car salesman from a college town could look so natural in this wild setting. He is undeniably handsome and, although he probably knows it, I like that he doesn't flaunt it. Sandy blond, medium-length, wind-blown shaggy hair. A strong jaw showing some stubble. Straight, clean teeth. His wide, genuine smile definitely shows those teeth. He's got a well-proportioned six-foot frame. He probably feels at home in any setting. I sense real compassion for others. And I know he has a good sense of humor and appears well liked by his friends. Of the three strangers living in the camp next door, Billy is the most appealing. Maybe we're both cut from the same mold.

"I should have thought to bring you guys each a sandwich and a beer," I said.

"Why do that, Stacey? This is your vacation too. I'm

sure you didn't leave the comfort of home to come here and continue doing the stuff that you would do there. My advice is, let your hair down. And by the way, your hair looks really nice here in the sun, shining so much. You give this wilderness some class."

"Thanks. But the fact that you noticed my hair lets me know that I was looking pretty ragged before, or maybe it's just that you're seeing the real me for the first time. Either way, it's nice that you noticed. Cynthia and I bathed this morning and washed our hair, and in all honesty, I wish I could just go native. This river water is too cold to try that again. So when you see me return to that ragged state, just remember that I clean up well."

"Don't worry, Stacey. Dirty or clean, it's nice to have you around."

I could tell our conversation was bordering on getting too personal, so I changed the subject. "Actually, I'm looking to see how Harry is doing. Is he much further up-river?"

"Not much further. Mind if I walk with you?" Billy said. "I could use a break from this spot."

Without waiting for an answer, he slogged out of the water and removed his waders.

Oh, dear. I'm in a quandary. Do I watch him or not? Although I am almost certain he's wearing jeans or some kind of pants under the waders, I'm not certain. I feel self-conscious being alone with this attractive man undressing in front of me in a secluded setting. Yet it seems perfectly natural, as if it were a logical thing to do. Okay, throwing decorum to the wind, I watch him undress.

I exhale slowly. Fortunately, Billy is wearing jeans under those waders. When he applied the final tug, balanced on one bootless foot, he hopped a short, backward, one legged dance and toppled over. Luckily, I was there to catch him and break the fall by hugging him from behind.

"That's why my daughters call me Grace," said my smiling catch. "Let's go find Harry."

"Well, Grace, if you didn't have any pants on under those waders, I wouldn't have caught you," I said. "Your ass would have hit the ground."

"I'd never have thought I'd be grateful to be wearing pants in your presence," Billy said and turned to lead the way along the path.

I provided emphasis to his pace with a swift kick to the back of his jeans and a not so stifled giggle. Yep, cut from the same mold all right.

Harry was so intent watching the man in the water that he didn't hear Billy and me until we were upon him. Sitting on the bank with his borrowed fly rod cradled on his lap, Harry started to rise but we told him to stay where he was. Billy and I sat down beside him and it seemed as though this was a spot the three of us often shared together. Three people from different households sitting on a riverbank in an idyllic setting watching a man in the water doing what he obviously loved doing.

"I was practicing my casts and after a while I saw Twin coming down the river. I wanted to ask him questions and have him evaluate my style, but he said if I really wanted to acquire the best technique I should find Chief and watch everything he does."

"He's right, Harry," Billy said. "Chief doesn't waste movement and he seems more at home in a river than anywhere else. If you're starting out and want to learn good habits, he's the one to watch."

"Aunt Stacey, I can't believe his rituals. After moving to each new spot, he thanks and honors all of life in that area. The fish, animals, birds, all the plants, then, after nodding to the four directions, he wets his tongue with the water. When he catches a fish, he blesses it and thanks it, wishing it a good life in the future. He really believes he is just another form of life on this river and that he has no more or less significance than any other form. I know my parents would never understand this, but I feel more spiritual here, watching him, than I ever felt in church."

Billy and I remained with Harry longer than we

intended, but we all seemed happy to pass the time together. Billy seemed reluctant to leave without me. We all seemed to enjoy the silence.

I watched Chief fish, and pray, and exist as a natural part of the scene, not an intruder. To anyone watching us, it probably looked like the three of us sitting on the riverbank were a contented family enjoying a beautiful performance.

I hated to break the reverie, but a low level of guilt began to build when I thought about leaving Cynthia in camp far longer than I had originally intended. So with a reluctant farewell to Chief and Harry, I returned Billy to his pole and waders.

I had no interest in watching Billy dress. In fact, I've never had any interest in watching a man dress. Dressing is anticlimactic, so why pay much attention to it?

"Why don't you guys come to our camp tomorrow for a chili dinner? I need to make a trip to town tomorrow, so I'll pick up the extra stuff I'll need. And if you're not sure, just ask Cody. I make a mean chili con carne."

"I think I can speak for the other two. The answer is yes. Good deal," said Billy.

Later that evening, after dinner, Billy strolled into

our camp. "Chili sounds like a great idea to all of us," he said, "but only if you let us bring bread and beer. I've been elected to go into town tomorrow and we agreed, if you want to go with me, I should drive because I know where to get everything we need. If that's alright with you guys."

"Well then, I guess that's settled," I said as the rest of my campmates looked at me with question marks in their eyes. I faced Cynthia and added, "It slipped my mind, but I offered to cook chili tomorrow for both camps. I forgot to tell you."

"Obviously, Billy didn't forget," said Cynthia. "But that sounds like fun. Tonight we can make a list of what we'll need and I'll watch you make your chili recipe, start to finish."

"Mom is not the greatest cook, but her chili's the best," Cody said. "You guys will be farting like crazy tomorrow night."

That was a compliment, I think.

"Then it's settled," said Billy. "Someone come get me tomorrow anytime you're ready. Round trip to town, including the shopping, is probably two or three hours."

After Billy left and we washed our dinner equipment stored it back in the SUV, Cynthia and I sat at the picnic table to plan.

"What do we need for the rest of the week, besides the chili ingredients?" asked Cynthia.

"More batteries for the flashlights. Ice. Firewood. Once I'm there, I'll look around and if anything pops up, I'll get it," I said.

In a nutshell, that's my typical approach to planning. I've never been interested in agonizing over details in advance, because nothing ever works out exactly as planned. Cynthia is more comfortable making lists, but she's not inclined to throw a dinner party in the first place. A shopping trip without Cynthia will take less time and require far less planning. I think I know Billy well enough now and together, he and I can work even faster. He'll know what the guys need and between the two campsites, we'll have everything covered.

"I sure wish I could buy Harry waders and whatever they wear for fly-fishing," Cynthia said. "But I didn't bring enough money. Anyway, I'll need to talk to Loren first about that. I've never seen my son so enthused about anything before. His time with Chief sure has had a marvelous effect."

That night, before sleep overtook us, I broached a topic with Cynthia that probably has more to do with my own self-evaluation. I know that no details of my behavior these last few days have escaped Cynthia's watchful eyes. In an effort to deflect her unspoken thoughts, I decided to face what was making me feel uncomfortable.

"Cynthia, I know you're being polite by not

questioning me about why I made plans for tomorrow without consulting you," I said. "It was a spur of the moment decision when talking to the men. Later on, I figured we should re-stock our food supplies and that I would go into town alone so that you could remain here with the boys. One of us should. I didn't realize Billy wanted to come along with me. I'll be fine driving to town tomorrow with him. I trust him. He's somewhat of a goof, but he's transparent. He might be attracted to me, who knows, but I've met dozens like him and they are easy to handle. Furthermore, I think you should spend time at the river watching Harry fly-fish. He would be proud to share his interest with you and it would provide good quality time alone with him."

I hope it didn't sound like I was implying Cynthia wasn't spending enough time with Harry. I hope I didn't sound like a meddler.

"I really admire your courage, Stacey. You're not afraid to live a full life. I would not have invited these new friends for a dinner in our space without Loren first giving his approval. It feels somewhat risqué to extend ourselves without our husbands here, but I agree—the men seem like good guys and the boys like them. This trip is full of new experiences."

"For me too, Cynthia," I said.

"I don't want to look back and think this could have been a better trip if only I'd let down my guard more. I want to take full advantage of our time here and not worry about anyone's motives. You're a good example of that, and anyway I have three family members here to help me expand my horizons. We're probably safe."

"I'll be just fine doing the shopping tomorrow morning while you spend time with Harry," I reassured her. "I look forward to preparing the chili dinner with you when we reconvene in the afternoon."

"Sounds good, Stacey," Cynthia said. "Goodnight."

I turned off my flashlight and snuggled in my sleeping bag. But my thoughts continued to whirl. My words to Cynthia about the trip into town with Billy tomorrow were far more confident than I feel, but that's nothing new. I have always been blessed—or damned—by being a risk-taker, but fortunately, I have strong survival skills. It's something I admire about myself. But have I pushed that trait too far? I often leap first, before looking, and don't I always land feet first?

I'm surprised I'm even thinking about my motives now. What does it mean that I'm questioning myself? Do I feel guilt? Do I feel shame?

I'd better not go there. Change the topic, I tell myself.

I am a considerate person and my good intentions protect me. Good karma had its advantages.

What is Cynthia thinking in the darkness next to me? Something about her reticence, but willingness to go beyond her comfort level intrigues me. She's been taught to be wary of anything new and to always seek out advice when faced with change. Decisiveness is not her strong point. She said she likes to keep life simple because it's easier that way, and detests disagreements, even in their mildest form.

I couldn't live like that. To me, that would be abandoning life. Far less interesting.

Cynthia's recent words about "expanding my horizons" rang in my mind, and that gives me hope for my sister-in-law. Maybe she feels her lifestyle has become too confining. Am I a good example of the alternative? Lord knows, I have often taken the other extreme to its limits. Cynthia and I could probably benefit by a move toward the middle.

# Twenty-Seven: Cody

"HARRY, WHY DON'T YOU GET A LIFE and think for yourself for a change?" We were in our tent and the words just erupted from my mouth.

"I don't know what you're so pissed about, Cody, but you've been in a bad mood all day. What is it? Did I do something wrong?"

"You glom onto whatever interests someone else," I said. "Those guys are into fly-fishing, so now you act as if it's the only way in the world to fish. I'm sick of you following those guys around like they know everything. Is it a gay thing with you? Because if it is, let me know now before we get to rooming together."

"You're crazy, Cody. I like fly-fishing and I happen to think that those guys in the next campsite know a lot more about it than you do, that's all. I plan to take advantage of what they teach me and if you can't handle that, I don't know what to say."

"Just don't expect me to go sniffing up their ass like you do, that's all."

"Go to sleep, Cody," said Harry.

Jeez, that kid makes me angry. I had planned to show Harry how to appreciate this wilderness but things are not going that way. Harry ignores me even though I'm so competent in this environment. I figured Harry would be more competent than me in school, but he's going to those other guys for advice. I shouldn't let him aggravate me like this. And then he has the balls to tell me what I should do, like he's trying to shut me up.

"And don't tell me to go to sleep," I called out into the darkness.

# *Twenty-Eight: Stacey*

EVEN BEFORE I OPENED MY EYES, my thoughts were riveted on Billy. The anticipation of spending hours alone with someone new, someone attentive. I know Billy likes the way I look, but I hope he is impressed with more than that. It's so exciting to know I can still attract someone who is smart and interesting. He's charming, too, and I do take delight in the art of allure. I wonder how much longer that is going to matter to me, now that I'm entering my fourth decade.

I'm trying to keep focused on Billy's infatuation with me and ignore my attraction to him. If I think about that, I'll feel guilty. But a spark has definitely ignited deep inside of me. There's no rational thought down there and I think I'd be all right if I keep that spark in my gut and out of my mind.

Cynthia is stirring, stretching, yawning.

"He's becoming his own man," Cynthia said, her eyes

still closed. "I don't know where he learned to do that, but I approve. You're right, Stacey. I need to show Harry that I support his new endeavors, whatever they are. He is about to branch out on his own and although Loren might not approve of his independence, Harry needs to know that I do."

That's good to hear. If she spends time with Harry today while I go to Enterprise for groceries, I bet her son will entertain her far more than that book she's reading.

&

"If you don't mind, I'd feel more comfortable driving my own car, but I'll need your help navigating," I said to Billy. "When Cody drove us here I didn't pay attention to the route."

"I'm comfortable with you driving," said Billy. "And glad that I'm needed. Just be sure to follow *all* my directions."

"Calm down, Marine," I cautioned.

The boys had already taken off with the rods and poles for the river, and Cynthia was reading her book. She planned to join Harry after a bit. No one seemed concerned that Billy and I were driving off together.

The beautiful landscape and the scents of the forest captured my attention. The sunlight filtering through the trees created a lovely pattern of light and dark and a full pallet of green hues—from dark, luxuriant forest denseness, to gentle feathery pistache moss. The road followed the Lostine River and all I could think of was—this is paradise.

The gravel road dropped in elevation for several miles and neither of us spoke. I was content in the silence. No need for nervous small talk. After a while, though, I thought I'd better check in with him.

"I hope I didn't hurt your feelings back there when I suggested that you calm down. I was just being playful," I said.

"No, Stacey, I understood that. I'm just kicking back. I feel real comfortable with you. By that, I mean I don't have to sell myself to you. You're easy to be with, and that's rare. Sure, I could ramble on about cars, or chitchat about almost any topic, but I'm content being silent in your presence."

My God! Is he reading my mind?

"Me, too," I said. "Sometimes you meet someone and it seems like you've known them forever. Getting to know their history doesn't seem important. It's like you can skip all that and just be—as if the two people are picking up from where they last left off, long ago."

Uh oh. Maybe I'm getting too deep into philosophy. So I changed course by saying, "What do you like with your chili? I'll pick up stuff to make a salad, but I can't bake cornbread on the fire, so how about rolls or tortillas or something?"

"Let's see if there's any good looking bread," Billy suggested. "Personally, I love baguettes."

"Then baguette it is, if they have it."

I followed the river road out of the mountains and into the hamlet of Lostine where I took a right turn and headed for the town of Enterprise, which is large enough for a grocery store and a fishing supply shop.

I pulled into the grocery first. It's fun to shop with someone new. Billy and I walked the aisles together, making menu decisions and selecting items. Compromise was needed, but we did it without bickering, and I had fun. We probably looked like a goofy couple having a good day.

There was a playfulness about how we interacted, and we stayed together the whole time rather than separately wandering the aisles. I enjoyed being near Billy and liked that it left me feeling pleasantly energized.

We argued over who would pay when we approached the cashier. I won by saying it was my idea to make the chili, and besides, my extended family had been borrowing supplies from Billy for days.

We were loading the grocery bags into my car when Billy said, "Hey, Stacey, I've got an idea. Please hear me out before you respond. You've used your gas and paid for the groceries, so let me offer something in return. I need to spend a half-hour at the fly shop and while I'm there, I'd like to pay for a hotel room with a shower so you can indulge yourself while I'm busy."

"Are you crazy? A room just to take a shower?"

"It wouldn't cost much more than you just spent on food. And when you're done, I would like a shower too. I must smell terrible."

"I don't know, Billy. I'd very much love a shower. I tried bathing in the river but it is too cold to do that again. Besides, how would that look?"

"Look to whom? It won't take much time and I'll be gone, shopping for fishing stuff anyway."

"You're a nut, Billy. Are you sure the motel rooms aren't expensive?"

"This isn't peak tourist season. It's no problem. I'm not suggesting that you *need* a shower and I'll shut up about it if you prefer, but I could use one and I thought it might be a nice indulgence for you, too. There are rooms a short walk from the fly shop."

"Well, I guess, if you insist, I could be done quickly while you're gone."

&

As soon as I entered the motel room, I told Billy to take-off, and he did. The room was not much, but it had a great shower. Alone in the room, with the door locked, I figured I had at least fifteen minutes of steaming hot luxury before Billy returned.

The hot water felt incredibly good, and although the motel shampoo and conditioner were not my preference, they did nicely. I had figured the timing about right because I had just finished redressing when I heard my benefactor knocking on the door.

"Are you decent?" Billy yelled from outside.

"I'm more than decent and always have been," I said. "Now it's your turn. Do you want me to leave so you can have some privacy?"

"No. Actually, I'd prefer it if you would join me," said Billy. He was fishing, but not for fish.

"Just be happy I don't drive away while you still have soap in your eyes," I warned as I turned on the TV and sat on the bed. "I'll be out here catching up on news. By the way, I used both towels, so you'll have to do with sloppy seconds."

"Women are the same everywhere," Billy said as he closed the bathroom door.

I began to work the tangles out of my hair with the comb I carry in my purse. The only thing I disliked was having to put on the same dirty clothes I had worn into the room.

Billy was in there a long time but finally I heard the shower water turn off. He exited the bathroom wearing only his jeans. He was barefoot. He carried his shirt.

"All right," I said. "I can see that you're buff. I'm

impressed. And just like your comment earlier about being like every other woman, you are like every other man. What is it you guys like so much about prancing around bare-chested in front of the opposite sex?"

Laughing, Billy said, "You got me pegged, but I bet you didn't realized how pleasant it was to share your towel. It still had your nice smell on it."

"Don't do that Billy," I replied. "That's too sweet."

I could feel my eyes glazing over, just a little. I may have smiled, which I hadn't meant to do. In spite of my better judgment, something inside me melted. Time slowed down and then stopped.

If the eyes are windows to something deep inside, then Billy read me easily. Not a word was spoken but we knew we were rushing in a direction neither wanted to avert. Apparently, it was worth the gamble.

Billy stepped closer to me and placed his hands on my waist. He pulled me gently to him. I watched his face intently until he was too close for me to focus. By then, I could do nothing but close my eyes and kiss him. There was passion coming from both sides.

After that first kiss, the press of damp bodies and clean, wet hair… my ability to stop was compromised. I fell over the cliff and abandoned the idea of retreat as our tongues and hands found each other.

It was one pleasurable touch after another, as if we pushed in all our chips and rushed into deep sensuality. I felt like a teenager with an unbridled libido, and the benefit of twenty-five years of sexual experience.

Our first embrace fused our bodies and we ungracefully made it over to the bed. The energy was strictly physical, entirely self-centered, and over-all exciting. Billy's erection was apparent from the first touch of our lips. Far from embarrassed by it, he seemed rather proud.

Apparently, he wanted the moment to last until he could stand no more because his focus was on me and my pleasure. And I let him. He undressed me slowly and paid attention to my responses. I was catapulted to a place beyond thought. A fleeting thought that I would rationalize my behavior later interrupted for just a second, but I went right back to that unconscious place of intense pleasure. If this was a one-time occurrence, I didn't want to leave anything on the table.

Lost in my own passion, I paid little attention to the man I was with. The physical energy brought on a flood of sexual feelings that I hadn't experienced in quite some time. I became the rebellious young woman who had tempted fate in my youth. The girl who abandoned all decorum to please herself and celebrated her independent spirit. Again, I felt the extreme excitement and mindless sensuality I had often longed for since then.

I couldn't have chosen a better playmate than Billy because I didn't have to give him much thought. I focused on my own pleasure. For a moment, my husband, Coach, surfaced, and it was as if I was sharing the forbidden passion with him. Maybe that's my way of lessening shame or guilt, because in my imagination I was making wild, physical love with the man I married years ago, prior to children and adult responsibilities.

Orgasm has always been easy for me and the first one occurred early, unleashing spasms of pleasant physical warmth. The urgency of our sex dictated changes in position, which allowed for further release with varying degrees of intensity. Each release was mine alone, unshared with my partner, yet to his great credit, he was able to maintain his poise through this whole unexpected occurrence. His restraint must have been a caring decision. Which pleased me. Unlike most other men, including my husband, Billy was willing to delay his consummate moment until I consented. With a sexual fervor that flushed through my body and because I was satisfied, I was finally ready to concentrate on him and his finale.

Our bodies were so in sync, that Billy sensed my readiness and turned his focus to his own enjoyment. It didn't take him long. When his orgasm began, I was sure he'd agree the delay had been worth it.

Once finished, and exhausted, we relaxed in quiet contemplation and then looked at each other and burst out laughing. The gate was completely open and everything inside had been released.

"I definitely need to take another shower," I said. "I smell like sex."

"Let's shower together," Billy suggested.

"Not on your life, you rooster."

&

The ride back to the campground was quiet, but we both had a smile on our face, glints in our eyes, and a lovely memory. But we didn't know what to talk about. I knew our friendship would end in a couple of days—the moment we left for home. I had no illusion about making any lifestyle changes. Yet I couldn't help but grin, thinking about what we had just shared. It felt like a really strong sexual dream.

"If anyone wonders why we took so long, tell them we were halfway back to camp when we realized we'd forgotten the beer," I said. "No one will complain about that."

"I don't think we took too much extra time," said my partner in crime. "It was wild and fun, but not something I would dare tell my friends. And I won't do anything that could embarrass either of us. You are here with family, and as far as I'm concerned, I'm nothing more than your new friend. We're actually more like brother and sister than lovers."

"You are nothing like my brother, Loren, who is Cynthia's husband. But I know what you mean," I said. "You and I seem very much alike. At least as far as two people of the opposite sex can be."

I steered my SUV into the camp area, and to my relief, no one else was around.

# Twenty-Nine: Twin

"UNFORTUNATELY, OUR SPECIES has grown to such numbers that we compete with other animals and plants for space, food, and water," I said as I nursed my second bowl of chili. "There's plenty of fights these days between neighbors over using our waterways for irrigating farm and ranch land, and keeping it natural for fish and drinking water."

A spirited conversation about Northwest ecology was taking place around the campfire.

"At the time of creation, God instructed man to rule over the lesser forms of life," Cynthia stated. "Man was created with the intellect to do that, and Eden was the location chosen for the first man to rule over all but God and his Angels. However, in Genesis, Adam and Eve met Satan in the form of an animal—a snake—and we all know the rest of that story. Satan didn't take the form of another human; he took the form of a snake. Animals should never be given preference over man."

"Well, Mom, that's one view, but I would like to think that God gave to man the role of *steward* over all life. Not to punish animals, use them, or look down on them in any way. God gave man the brains to make sure all His creatures are protected and given a chance to thrive. I think man's God-given intelligence is misused by many people who take advantage by selfishly profiting from other forms of life and therefore do not protect them. I would like to study Ecology at college so that I can be at the forefront of that effort of protection."

I think Harry is up to the task of blending the science of evolution and ecology with his strong biblical knowledge. But Billy and Chief avoided the debate as it drifted into the differences between science and the Bible. Chief brought the conversation around.

"Harry, I appreciate your concept of steward," Chief said. "It implies a role different than boss or ruler. I believe all life has the same right to space on this Earth that I do. I don't want to remove an animal or a plant just because it's in my way. At the same time, I want to ensure that the needs of all living things are met. To do that, my role is to decide what's best for all, which could easily result in a superior or biased attitude unless I constantly remind myself that I am just another of the life forms and my role is protector, not boss. I keep myself reminded of that by blessing all life that is in the space near me. If I need food or shelter, it will likely be provided by something living that can fulfill that need, so I acknowledge and bless that life for its contribution. If I take something I need, I then look to replace it for the good of all. It is a cycle that I hope will continue. When my life is spent, other life will make use of what I leave. My remains will promote their life. We have been given the knowledge by a Great Spirit to be able to do that for the preservation of ourselves and of all life."

"I agree with Chief," I said. "We humans adjusted our environment for ourselves. We can buy everything we need in a store. But it seems we've distanced ourselves from the rest of life, to the detriment of all life. We don't see or touch a live salmon—we see and touch a fillet wrapped in plastic. We don't personally fall a tree to build our house or fence—we buy boards at a hardware store. I think everyone would benefit from spending time in the wilderness, just like your family is doing. I worry that we've grown so removed from the rest of life that we can't relate to the beauty and the rights of all those other life forms. If being distant is the way man chooses to live, then we'll soon run out of everything. Thank God for the stewards who watch and warn."

Cynthia rustled her son's hair and bent to take his empty bowl. She beamed when she said, "I'm proud of Harry's decision to study science in college. His father's not so sure it's a good choice, but maybe now I can talk to him about the concept of stewardship and the role Harry will play in God's work. His father puts too much emphasis on predestination, which may come from laziness or perhaps even fear. What you men say makes sense, but it isn't how I've been taught. It's hard for me, and somewhat scary, to change old ideas."

"I don't care what Dad says," Harry said. "I think all that predestination crap is a cop-out. I think God's will is for us all to survive, including the least among us, which is probably some single-celled plant."

"Got my vote, Harry," I said, winking.

# Thirty: Stacey

CODY'S DISINTEREST IN THIS TOPIC motivates me to search for something else to discuss with him. I can count on Billy to join in with us because he's not paying attention to the conversation; he's been staring at me the whole evening.

Cody had formed a bond with Billy, more so than with the two other men, so he didn't seem to notice anything odd when Billy sat down next to him.

The other men seem more serious, and maybe more goal-oriented. Billy has a devil-may-care attitude. It must have occurred to Cody that he and Billy think alike, so it's only natural they would be comfortable with each other.

Before I could find a subject of interest, Cody blurted out, "We're all animals, and it all comes down to survival of the fittest. Humans seem to be the fittest, so, until that changes, we make the rules on this planet. It's easy to say we understand a lofty goal, but in the end, we all revert to our animal ways when we want something. Far from stewards, we're more like scavengers."

I think Cody feels better after providing a counter-punch to his cousin's highfaluting philosophy. My son will never allow Harry to gain ascendancy over him. I guess Cody wants us to know that he is a fit animal and will survive just fine.

I glanced at Billy and couldn't stifle a smile. He returned the grin. Does Cody know?

No. My fear of that was erased when Cody said, "The people in this camp are able to act as higher animals, but I don't think most people can. In the third world there are new societies springing up that don't want to be outdone by richer nations, so they're doing damage we can't control and that might eventually ruin it for us all."

"Does that mean we shouldn't do our part to help stem the disaster?" I asked. "What about the stuff we do right here in our rich nation, just to make us richer?"

"Harry gives the impression that ecology is the noble thing to do," Cody said. "But I think the greater good comes from politicians and educators who carry the message to those doing the most damage. Harry's goal seems like the Dutch boy with his finger in the dike. I don't want to dis that work completely, but let's not make it sound like it's the whole answer."

"Cody makes a good point about educating the others on the planet," said Billy. He directed that statement to me, but it was meant for Cody. "Maybe his role in life will be to inform others through lecture or writing or something like that. I would think Cody is well suited for travel and leaving behind a good impression on people different from us. He talks about survival of the fittest and it seems to me that his calling might be to influence people. In my opinion, so much of life is selling yourself and your opinions. Nothing major happens until someone convinces others to act. If I remember right, Stacey, you said your husband is a teacher and coach, a perfect example of a person who motivates students by first selling himself. I think Cody has those same gifts and if he chooses to use them, he'll be as noble as anyone."

Cody smiled when he heard Billy's words and validation. My son is a sucker for praise and I know that all the attention focused recently on Harry is hard for him to take. I'm as proud of Cody as I am of his cousin and I showed him by looking directly at him, giving him a smile, and nodding in agreement.

I was also silently praying that my lust was out of my system. There is no reason to ever try that again.

By dawn of the sixth day, both camps had settled into routines that took little thought and even less discussion. As usual, the boys rose earlier than Cynthia and I, and started a fire. By the time it was crackling, we began to stir and then moan loudly for coffee, which the boys were only too happy to oblige. Making the coffee was necessary to get Cynthia and me in motion, but once we were up, the boys' duties were over. It was our job to make breakfast.

The men in the camp next door were early risers. Their coffee was long finished, and they were somewhere on the river. The men were so silent in the morning that we were never disturbed.

Would our sons become early risers one day?

"You guys are getting better and better at producing a great first cup," Cynthia said, standing by the fire in her sweatpants. She was gripping a cup in both hands as if she was cold, or possibly afraid someone would try to take it from her.

As the week progressed, Cynthia and I became less concerned with the vanity of looking good when we emerged from our tent. Comfort in the forest freed us from superficial concerns. Our mornings consisted of a leisurely, but hearty cooked breakfast and discussion about the day's plans. Harry was happy to fly-fish with Twin's extra rod and station himself near enough to Chief to observe him cast.

Cody enjoyed his spinning rod, and began taking his drawing tablet to the river to work on his cartooning when taking a break from fishing. It had been quite a while since I saw him so energized about his art. I think his inspiration seems to increase during periods of emotional upheaval. Someday soon, when his emotions are more stable, I'll point out my observation to him. I imagine Cody's impending departure from home, starting college, forging a relationship with Harry as his roommate, and all the unknowns—are responsible for his anxiety. But I'll wait for some later time to share my thoughts with him.

I'm feeling pretty contented in the woods. Hiking or jogging is something I've done almost every day here, sometimes with Cynthia, but mostly alone. I like to spend part of every day by myself. There are numerous trails emanating from the river and I've learned to be relaxed in the wilderness for at least a half-mile in all directions. With my men stretched along a mile or so of river, I feel safe because I'm always within vocal reach of somebody. The late morning or afternoon hikes fulfill my goals of exercise and exploration. I have always been health and body conscious.

My solitary walks make it easy for me to check in with the guys when they're fishing. I don't think my presence bothers them. They probably view me as an interlude and look forward to my arrival. I enjoy hearing their stories. Especially from Billy.

I also check in every day with Harry and I'm so happy to see his enthusiasm regarding his new hobby. He said his fly-fishing skills are improving, which makes him even more dedicated to practice. If we stay here much longer, I fear he might just move in with the men from Oregon and become part of their camp.

However, my most enjoyable time has been with Cody. He shows me his drawings and tells me about the fish he's caught but released back into the river. I share his sense of pride. Our visits along the riverbank are unlike anything else I've done with him in the eighteen years of his life. Sure, I've knocked on his closed bedroom door and inserted myself into his domain, usually to inspect it, but this is different. We've started a new future together where we're learning to visit and share with each other in a mature way.

Cynthia is happy to take a casual walk with me, but she has no interest in power hiking. She likes to remain in camp—reading, or straightening up our living quarters, or preparing sandwich fixings for lunch and planning hot dinners.

Our individual routines are comfortable and well defined. We no longer feel like immigrants on a foreign shore. We're compatible, and confident in this wild environment. I would love to stay here indefinitely. Harry, too.

&

"Well! Look who's here!" I shouted to Cynthia as I washed our breakfast dishes.

Because his hybrid sedan makes so little noise, I was totally surprised when Loren drove his Prius into our campsite. He parked next to my SUV.

Cynthia stood up so quickly, she became entangled in the frame of her camp chair, nearly tripping over it as it collapsed around her. Loren didn't notice because his attention was focused on scanning the campground.

I haven't seen my brother in almost two years. He's always been clean-shaven, but now he's showing some gray in what little hair he has left, mostly above his ears. Like our father, he's bald on top, but letting his remaining hair grow long and wispy, which is so like Dad that I find it somewhat eerie.

"What are you doing here, Loren?" Cynthia said. "I thought you were in Boise, working."

"It's Saturday, or have you been here so long that you've lost track of time? I left work early yesterday and thought I'd surprise you last night, but couldn't find you. I hate not having cell phone access with you. I drove up and down this road last night, but not this far into the wilderness. Where is Harrison?"

"He and Cody are on the river, fishing," I said.

"Oh! Hi, Stacey," Loren said. Then he hesitantly

approached and gave me a cursory, brotherly hug.

Loren circled the campsite, apparently inspecting our living quarters. Then he sat down and resumed his travel tales. "I drove up this road last night, before dark looking for this place. I remembered you said you planned to camp somewhere on the Lostine River and I guess I envisioned a large campground with showers and all. Obviously, I saw nothing like that. Only these little sites with no amenities and nobody camping anywhere. After a while, I turned back thinking that you'd not want to get so remote. When I got back out of the mountains, I asked people if they'd seen you, but no one had."

"I'm sorry for all the trouble you went through, honey," said Cynthia, as if she was the cause of his distress.

"Finally, I went to Enterprise and because it was about to get dark I got a motel room. This morning, the manager told me that there were a few campsites further up than I had gone, so I set out determined to find you. My intention was to spend these last couple of days, which now turns out to be one night, camping with you. You were hard to find."

"Well, I'm glad you're here," said Cynthia. "Have you eaten yet today?"

I couldn't help but wonder if Loren stayed at the same motel and slept in the same bed that Billy and I had so wantonly used earlier in the day. "We would have put out bread crumbs for you to follow, Loren, if we'd only known," I joked.

Loren shot me a quick glance implying my comment was a smart-aleck interruption, and turned his attention back to his wife. "I ate a breakfast in town. Whose camp is that over there?"

"Those are three fishermen from Oregon who come here every year. They've been good neighbors, nice and respectful of our space," said Cynthia.

I wish Cynthia said they were wild mountain men and that we had tamed them by using mysterious feminine skills we generally keep bottled up. It might be good for Loren to wonder if there is a side to his wife that he doesn't know. In my opinion, Cynthia worries too much about his comfort and assuaging his fears.

That's not my style. I want to make Loren squirm. Keep 'em guessing, I say. But therein might lay my problem. I know that too often I think too much of my own enjoyment and not enough about how it affects others, especially those prone to be fearful. I take too many risks and I'm too self-absorbed, so I could use a small dose of Cynthia's self-restraint. Or maybe I just like to torture my brother.

"So those men must be on the river with our boys. Do they get in each other's way, or are they all playing together nice?" asked Loren.

When I listen carefully to his questions, I can tell he

made up his mind before anyone offers an answer. That is one reason why I always want to prove him wrong. It certainly didn't take long for him to get under my skin again.

"They've been great to the boys," said Cynthia. "In fact, Harry has taken a strong interest in the fly-fishing that they do and they've been teaching him about it. They even loaned him a spare pole."

Bad answer, I thought, but I love it. That comment won't help calm Loren down—it will just inflame his worry about the influence those strangers have on his son. Cynthia must know her husband feels threatened by all other men, especially those who capture Harry's attention. Loren knows he can't control outsiders.

Cynthia seems to be giving Loren too much credit for being sociable and normal, as if he is just like the middle-age men we've been getting to know this past week. Perhaps I, like Loren, might also be jaded and untrusting. After all, I'm judging Loren in the worst light.

"I'll go to the river and see for myself how these men are getting along with the boys."

That's when I noticed Loren had a handgun underneath his jacket—tucked in between his left arm and torso. I'd forgotten he never goes anywhere unarmed.

Ever since he was eighteen, Loren has carried a weapon. Although he was always attentive to gun safety, and is an expert shot, he's got such a distrustful personality that it worries me. In fact, Loren's gun was the excuse I gave my parents as the reason I left home. I knew they would rather accept my departure than question my older brother's decision to carry a weapon. Growing up, whatever the problem, Loren, at the top of the pecking order, would always win.

My actions for the past twenty-five years have been dictated by a desire to create for myself a preferred status in my own family arrangement. I've positioned my life so that my vote carries as much weight as any other person's vote. Early on, I decided no male would ever have the power to cause me guilt or shame again. Not that I want dominion over anyone else, but I demand a role of equality and respect for my opinions. Seeing my brother today helps me realize that I have successfully accomplished the goal I set when I was sixteen. I still detest my older, crazy brother and his gun.

Cynthia helped Loren unpack what little gear he brought—toiletries, sleeping bag, beer. The latter he had apparently been drinking during his morning search for us. Although anxious to see Harry, Loren was hesitant to head to the river without his wife—and another beer.

"I'll take you to where I think Harry is and I know he'll be happy to see you," said. Cynthia. "Of course, I am, too."

I decided to join them.

"Hey, Dad!" said Harry as we came into view. "I didn't know you'd be coming here."

"What's the matter, Harrison, don't you want me to be here?" asked his father.

"No, no. Don't get me wrong, I'm glad to see you. Anyway, I want you to meet Chief here. He's with Oregon Fish and Wildlife, but on vacation like us."

The two men waved to each other but Chief didn't seem particularly interested in navigating the water that separated them.

"Your son is showing signs of a fly-fishing addiction and I can appreciate that," shouted Chief across the span.

"Well, Chief, I hope he doesn't become too addicted because he starts college next week and he'll need to focus all his attention on that."

Never one to avoid an opportunity to talk to his son through another person, Loren continued, "It'll be important for him to set aside his new fishing interest and buckle down to important, real-life pursuits. But I'm glad that he's had some diversion before engaging in the demands of a college semester."

"There was a time, not that long ago, when fishing was the most important chore people could do," countered Chief. "Personally, I like keeping that silly legacy alive."

It was too late to take this conversation down a different track, and since Chief was in the river and

Harry on the bank, it was easy for him to direct his father down the path to a spot where they could sit and talk.

Cynthia and I followed as they walked along the river. I thought about how Harry had taken the week's opportunity to befriend men from different backgrounds and beliefs than he'd grown up with. Opinions were accepted, and respect demonstrated by not trying to change minds or make fun of each other's interests. I figure those dynamics will change, now that Loren is here.

"Chief and his friends have been very respectful of us and protective," said Harry. "Since they've been to this place so often, they know what to bring. They have set routines and are considerate of other campers. They've shared supplies that we forgot, but otherwise have kept their distance. I've probably been closer to them than the others have, but that's because I'm interested in their type of fishing, and in Chief's line of work."

Oh, no, Harry! Be careful with that line of conversation with your dad.

"As far as college," Harry continued, "all three men have been very encouraging to both Cody and me."

His father surprised me.

"It's nice that we have this time to talk, Harrison. And that topic is appropriate. You'll soon be on your own. Decisions about who to trust, and who not to, will be solely yours. I hope the time you've spent with your mother and me will pay off. The world is good, but it can also be vicious, and I hope you will withhold your trust in people until you have ample evidence of their motives. The only people you can be completely sure of are yourself and your family. I'm not even sure Cody is someone you can trust. No offense, Stacey." Loren said, turning to me.

What Loren was saying was meant for all of us, not just for Harry. I shook my head in amazement. Loren is so arrogant. I'm happy Harry will soon be rid of him.

"All I ask, Harrison, is that you remain aware that people always think about themselves first. Self-interest is the great motivator. If your interests further theirs, then you are acceptable, on their team, working toward their goals. If your interests are not aligned, then you are the enemy. That's why it's important to keep your guard up and always assess a person's motives."

This kind of conversation is so pleasurable for Loren. I remember how he would philosophize as a teen, but I certainly never appreciated it. Stifled by a dominant father and ignored by me, Loren had no audience in our home. I guess he remedied that problem by getting married and siring a son.

Harry sat there showing rapt attention and unfettered agreement. Obviously, he knows anything short of that will create tension and even more emotional distance. Harry respectfully allows his father to philosophize *ad nauseum*, and he probably knows it matters even more when Loren states it in front of his wife and sister, even though we have heard it all before.

I think Harry is old enough to decide for himself how much of his father's advice to leave on the riverbank.

Cynthia, as a diversion, suggested lunch.

As we headed back to camp, Loren seemed invigorated, proud to be the wise father and the head of his strong nuclear family.

"I think I'll go look for Cody," I said. I had already spent enough time with my brother's family.

# Thirty-One: Harry

WHEN DAD CRACKED ANOTHER BEER I said, "Mind if I join you?"

Dad looked stunned and didn't answer right away. For years, I've watched Dad drink, always alone. He doesn't have any drinking buddies, but perhaps I can fill that role.

"Harrison!" Loren finally got out of his mouth. "Well, I guess that you are of legal drinking age and beer will be available in college and all. So, well, I guess, why not?"

I'm feeling very uncomfortable. There's no shared camaraderie, no ribald jokes. No laughter.

Dad has always been a solitary drinker and I know he uses it as an escape. Maybe having a drink with him infringes on his space somehow. But I don't care. I'm enjoying watching his discomfort. I couldn't care less about drinking this beer. I'd rather have a cola.

&

"Hello, folks," said Twin.

I hadn't noticed the three men as they crossed the boundary into our campsite. Pine needles have a wonderful way of muting forest sounds. Dad sure looked surprised.

"We thought we'd come over to welcome your dad, Harry," said Twin as he stuck out his hand to introduce himself.

"I met the Chief earlier," said Loren, "and have been told that the three of you have been kind to my family."

"I'm glad they think so. But his name is Chief—that's not a title, although he would probably would like it to be," laughed Billy. "Where's Cody and Stacey?"

I shrugged and offered the men a beer. They refused. Twin said their lunch was waiting in their camp. I caught a stern glance from Dad. He would never offer beer to strangers.

When the men departed, Dad glared at me. "Does this mean you'll start buying the beer? Because until that happens, I'll be the only one that offers it to others."

"I'm heading to the river to fish," I said.

# Thirty-Two: Loren

CYNTHIA AND I REMAINED IN CAMP while the others, who apparently chose to skip lunch, were out doing whatever they did along the river. Cynthia was prattling on, giving me a day-by-day account of her adventure, but I wasn't listening.

I don't know what to do out in the woods, so I fidgeted with things on the table, then cracked open another beer and began to pace.

"Loren, honey, you should have brought a book or something from work to occupy yourself," said my wife. "We can take a hike, or you're welcome to one of my books if you prefer."

"I can walk around or read back in Boise," I told her. "I don't need to come here to do that."

"Why don't you take a walk up the river to see Cody? I'm sure he'd like to spend some time with his uncle. He's probably hanging out near the others."

"By 'the others,' do you mean the men in the camp over there? You certainly make them sound like close friends. Has my unexpected presence ruined your plans with them?" I said.

"Loren! You're just being an ass. Go take a walk while I disregard what you just implied," said Cynthia.

"It's just that nobody is excited about seeing me and now I'm thinking it was a mistake to surprise my family. You all seem to be doing just fine here without me. I'm heading down to check out the river."

Where is the river? I wandered in the river's direction with no destination in mind. I have no intention of socializing with any of these people—family included. I'll never see those men again, and my sister and nephew might as well be strangers. Stacey dismisses me as if I'm inferior to her. Being around her again reminds me of why I'm better off when she's out of mind. Cynthia said Cody is upstream, probably with his prima donna mother, so I'll head downstream. I need some privacy.

# Thirty-Three: Stacey

BILLY AND I HAVE DONE A GOOD JOB keeping a respectable distance from each other. We've made sure never to be alone—there's safety in numbers. We act as if nothing has changed between us.

But can I trust myself? I don't want a repeat performance. Even though I do enjoy his company. And I would love more, as if we'd just gotten started, but I'm too afraid to say anything to him. When we depart for home tomorrow, a handshake will be laughable.

One more time alone with Billy would be better. It would give us time for an appropriate goodbye, better than an adios in a group setting. I could use the closure. This afternoon is probably our last chance to spend quiet time together. I should tell him I have no regrets. Yes. I'll do that now. I'll head over to where Billy is most likely to be fishing.

There must have been a synchronization of minds

because Billy said, "Want to take a walk downriver with me?" Billy asked. "We're all leaving soon and might not get another chance to talk, alone."

"All right," I replied. "Providing it's just talk you have in mind, Billy."

"Absolutely. What we shared yesterday is a great memory, and I don't want to spoil it. I hope you feel the same."

We began walking on the bank alongside the river. I was thinking about how bittersweet tomorrow's parting will be. I'll probably feel uneasy about Billy once I get home to Coach. And yet I already have the desire to see him again. But that would prove fatal to everything I hold dear. Physical distance will provide protection against further involvement and risky behavior. Our lives won't intersect ever again.

I wanted to take Billy's hand in mine, but of course, I didn't. That would make no sense. We're just ships passing in the night.

Billy's words interrupted my thoughts.

"Isn't life sometimes cruel? People ought to be able to live in their dreams until they're satisfied. Stacey, you and I will both move on, but I'm sorry our paths crossed for such a brief moment. "

"I agree," I said. "But we both have satisfactory lives in the real world. I don't want to complicate anything back there. We both have so much, but we could lose everything so easily. The excitement of seeing each other occasionally in the future doesn't balance the risk. I don't want to wind up hating you because you're a temptation I'm too weak to resist."

After a deep breath I said, "I'll be content, but not happy, to think of you far away, surrounded by your strong family and knowing that you are competently cared for by those you love."

I can't believe I just said that. I'm not even sure I mean it. Yes, it was the right thing to say, but that's not how I feel inside.

"I won't get a chance to kiss you later on and I really want to now," Billy said. "A handshake tomorrow will be for the benefit of the others, but it won't satisfy me."

Billy's request mirrored my feelings and I was happy to oblige. "Okay, but just a kiss. I mean that because I can't trust either one of us."

# Thirty-Four: Loren

I DON'T KNOW WHY I'M FEELING so unsettled. Where does this trail lead? Can I get lost if I just keep following the river? The others don't realize all the sacrifices I make for them and the vigilant oversight I provide. No one appreciates how hard I work to maintain that vigilance.

My wife and son have been swayed by the selfish pursuits of those men and their self-centered motives. Cynthia and Harrison will get hurt if no one stays alert to protect them. Why is my presence discounted and my advice ignored? It's my hard work and money that allows them to waste their time here. Where's the gratitude? Why do I have to be the steady one they use to springboard themselves into such frivolous distractions? Having mindless fun has never been an option for me. I bear the responsibility of making sure other people's fun stays within acceptable limits. Am I the only one who knows proper limits?

They must listen to me!

This trip is not my idea of a proper family rejuvenation and send-off for Harrison. My idea is... well, something different, but I don't know what. What I do know is that I would have been more in control of the setting and the company. Am I hearing voices?

Yes! People are talking up ahead. I didn't think anyone else was on this trail.

I hid behind a tree so as not to intrude when I saw my sister and one of the men from Oregon. How come she finds it so easy to develop friendships with men? This has been going on since our teens when she'd bewitch my friends with her so-called charms. They ask me to fix them up with her, but she never listened to me then. And she still doesn't listen to me. Why can't I let that go? Why can't I get Stacey out of my mind?

Plenty of girls have gotten my attention, so why do I still spend so much time thinking about Stacey? What's she got that makes men want her? Dad fawned over her, fondled her, and who knows what else they did behind closed doors. She never gave me any of what she gave him. Just the opposite. She played with Dad, but she treated me like shit. She repulses me. She makes me jealous. Why does she deliberately make me miserable? She's like a cat playing with a mouse. Like a spider, she's waiting for me to enter her web. There's nothing I can do but wait, and hope. I hate her. I desire her.

They're embracing! Look at her! Stacey is kissing that man! That's no friendly kiss—that's lust!

"What the hell is going on here?" I yelled.

Instantly, as if a spring latch had been released, Stacey and the man sprang apart.

"Loren! You're spying on us?" Stacey said. "What you just saw was a goodbye kiss between friends who will be departing tomorrow."

What a lame excuse. Who does she think she's kidding? "Bullshit!" I yelled back at her. "If I hadn't come walking down the path, you two would be getting it on in the bushes. I know you, you slut!"

"Hold on there, guy," Billy said. "Don't you call her a slut. What the ... is that a gun in your hand?"

"Damn straight, buddy," I said, "and if you don't get your ass the fuck out of here, I'll blow you away."

No one moved until Stacey said, "Billy, go ahead, I'll handle this. He's my brother, I'll be okay."

"You're sure?"

Stacey nodded. She was fearless.

Reluctantly, the guy edged around me but I never took my eyes off him. Cautiously, he walked backward for a while, then headed back down the trail toward camp.

"If you're concerned about her safety, you might want to just leave and keep your mouth shut about what just happened here, because this bitch doesn't mean as much to me as you think," I yelled as he disappeared around a bend.

"My turn, Stacey," I said. "If you think you can disrespect me and the rest of your family, you're mistaken. I want you on your knees." I put my pistol back in the shoulder holster.

"Are you crazy, you asshole? Stay out of my business and you can cram your opinions up your ass."

"Get on your knees and do what I want, or Cody and Coach will be the first to know what a slut you are."

I took the gun back out to emphasize my point. "I will take great pleasure in ruining your life," I told her.

"Okay, Loren," Stacey said, "but put that gun down." She knelt in front of me.

I put the pistol on a log and unzipped my pants. "You've done this for every man you've met. Now it's my turn! Long overdue."

"Screw you, asshole," she said.

That just inflamed me more. I grabbed her by the hair, close to her scalp, and forced her face up to my crotch and let my penis touch her skin.

But I remained flaccid. So I ground my crotch against her face to increase my arousal.

Stacey spit and started making a low growling noise.

She's not reacting like I expected. Why won't she do for me what she does for everyone else? Why won't she try to please me?

# Thirty-Five: Cody

BILLY SAID SOMETHING ABOUT TROUBLE with my mom, and a gun, and so his two Marine buddies, and Harry, and I followed as he ran along the river trail.

Uncle Loren had his back to us and was doing pelvic gyrations. Mom was on her knees in front of him, but she didn't seem to be in danger of death. That's when I realized what was going on.

Twin placed one hand over my mouth and the other across my chest, to keep me silent and calm. I wanted to rush out there and somehow stop Uncle Loren. Twin shook his head, no. I got the message—don't scare a crazy man.

But Harry rushed headlong at his father's back, an enormous primal scream erupting from his throat. He leapt at his father's back and the crashed took the wind out of his father. Harry's scream had sliced through the forest, reaching Cynthia, who was comfortably reading a book back in camp.

Twin let go of me and we all rushed to help Harry subdue his father. But Harry wouldn't stop pummeling him.

"Loren is unarmed!" Stacey called out. "The gun is over there!"

Harry was crying and shaking, but he continued to ferociously beat Uncle Loren with a vengeance I'd never have predicted. Uncle Loren wasn't even defending himself. He was cowering, protecting his head. Billy and Twin finally lifted Harry off his father.

Aunt Stacey was still pointing to the gun. Chief rushed to the pistol, grabbed the handgrip, and threw it forcefully into the middle of the Lostine River.

"It's bad enough that you pointed that gun at me, but you made your worst move by pointing it at Stacey," Billy said, his face up close to Loren's battered one.

I rushed over to Mom to make sure she was okay. When she stood up, we went over to Harry and put our arms around him. Harry was panting hard, still glaring at his father.

That's when Aunt Cynthia arrived. Her posture was rigid and she looked to be in shock. She was vigorously shaking her head, but seemed unable to speak.

"Chief got rid of the gun," Billy announced.

Then Loren stood up, stormed past his wife without even glancing at her, and rushed back to the campsite.

"Does he own any more guns?" Twin asked Aunt Cynthia.

"No. Loren is not a hunter. He carries only the one pistol," said Aunt Cynthia.

Harry nodded in agreement. He walked up to her, reached out his arms, and sobbed into his mother's shoulder.

"Are you all right, Stacey?" Billy asked.

"Yes," Mom answered. I still had an arm around her.

Harry's breathing eventually calmed and he let go of Aunt Cynthia. She spun around, and ran back down the path after her husband.

# Thirty-Six: Loren

WHEN I REACHED THE CAMPSITE, I cracked open a beer and began pacing. To calm myself. To slow my thoughts. When I saw my wife rush in, I knew I needed to take control and dictate how she must view this unfortunate mess from now on. My sister is a sinister bitch whose antics merit no one's respect. It was a relief to focus on conjuring up an explanation.

"I can't believe my own sister seduced me! She's sick. I should have seen it coming because she used to play sick games with me when we were teenagers. It's exactly the reason why she left home at seventeen. She couldn't keep her hands off me, or any other guy for that matter. She's been interested in one thing and one thing only all her life. She lives for sex. The nastier the better."

"Listen to yourself, Loren," my wife replied. "What are you saying? Are you crazy? Tell me what happened back there. No matter what you say, I don't know if I'll believe you. Harry was being comforted by Stacey; no one was helping you. Your face and clothes indicate you were in a fight. No one else has a split, bleeding lip and swollen eye."

"It wasn't my fault," I said. "I came upon Stacey and that other guy getting it on in the woods. When I confronted them, he ran away and she began coming on to me, begging me not to tell anyone. Soon the guy came back with his friends and they all jumped me, even Harrison. They've got Harrison spun against me to such an extent that he hit me. My lip's bleeding, yes, but my own son did that. How did things get so screwed up? Strange fishing friends are more important than his father? I'm getting out of here right now. Are you coming with me?"

"I'm not going to leave Harry behind! I need to talk to him, and to Stacey. In fact, I think we should all sit down and talk."

"I don't want to see either of them, so I'm not staying," I said. "I don't want to talk to my sister ever again. So I guess I'll see you and Harrison back home tomorrow."

I didn't want to leave my wife behind, beyond the bounds of my control, but I sure don't want to look at any of those people again. I can't count on Cynthia. Once again, my sister has turned everyone against me. She would have screwed that guy right there on the riverbank if I hadn't broken that up.

Staying here is dangerous. I'd better leave. I screwed up. I need to think. I will never ask for anyone's forgiveness. I will never say I'm sorry. To do so would weaken my reputation in the eyes of my wife and child.

My family is my only concern. My reputation is solid and I'm proud of myself. I've worked hard to make sure of that. I've backed up my words with action. Although I can't think of a way out of this problem right now, given time, I'll come up with a plausible explanation. Something my wife and son will believe. First, I need time to think.

My wife walked me to my car. She seemed to hesitate before leaning in the car window and giving me her half-hearted kiss goodbye. I started the engine and put the transmission into drive.

"You tell that son of a bitch Indian that I expect him to give you a check for seven hundred dollars to replace my pistol," I yelled. "Don't forget. Bring that check home with you tomorrow!"

Cynthia stood there as I drove off and I watched her in my rearview mirror. I think she was crying. I think that she regretted that kiss goodbye.

# Thirty-Seven: Stacey

WE REMAINED AT THE RIVER for about an hour after Loren and Cynthia left. The men said that in military circles, they call this process debriefing. Each person gets the opportunity to recount their feelings and the rest listen in a non-judgmental way. It took longer for Harry and me to calm down, but I think he and I benefited the most. Twin said it was to initiate the process of healing.

My heart was beating seriously fast after Loren attacked me and I needed time to calm down. No one seemed eager to move on. Confronting Loren again is the last thing I want, so when Twin suggested we talk about what just happened, I was relieved. I feel so sorry for Harry. I don't know what he's going to do when we go back to the campsite and he has to face his parents.

Billy has positioned himself far away from me but I've caught his glance a couple of times. I'm more concerned about him than I am for myself. I've been through this kind of thing with Loren before, and knew I would survive. Loren would never use that gun. But I think Cody and Billy are worried about me. There's no need. It was my poor choices that triggered Loren's behavior, and so this should be my burden to carry alone.

Billy didn't talk much. Maybe he wanted to hear what I said about how we happened to be on the riverbank together. He'd probably support anything I said, even if my version blamed him for everything. Blaming Billy might save my reputation, but I can't do that to him. I knew it was up to me to set the scene.

"At my suggestion," I began, "Billy and I took a walk and were talking about this week of camping and how nice it was to develop new friendships. This is a beautiful, wondrous place, and we've had a lot of laughs over the past week. I regret our time here will soon come to an end. So Billy and I were talking about how we'll lose touch with each other, but that is exactly how it should be. We all have lives and families that will keep us busy, but I thought it would be nice to talk privately with Billy, to say goodbye. I realize now that was a mistake because we shared a parting kiss and that is exactly when Loren approached us. I don't know how long he'd been watching us, but it couldn't have been for more than a minute or two."

I looked at Cody. He was sitting next to me, holding me close. His arm was around my shoulder.

"As inappropriate as it was, it was just that, a kiss on the lips, to denote my friendship and my goodbye. Anyway, your Uncle Loren got the wrong idea, and maybe he'd had too many beers. In any case, he drew his gun and chased Billy off."

Billy was probably relieved the story I told was the truth. Of course, I left out the details about the depth of our friendship, but those details were not needed.

So I continued. "Loren has always resented me. He also wants to control and humiliate me." Looking at Harry I said, "Your dad probably didn't really intend to do how it appeared. He misread what was happening between Billy and me and, reverting to his childhood, he wanted to teach his little sister a lesson. Loren is a very religious guy who believes punishing, in a very graphic way, is the answer to what he considers sin. What he was doing looked much worse than it was."

Harry gave me a half-hearted smile. Perhaps he didn't believe his father's behavior was justified, and perhaps he knew I didn't either. Yet the boy looked relieved with the version I offered. It's easier for all of us to live with that one. I suspect Harry's life has changed in a major way this afternoon.

That's when Twin grabbed Billy's arm and said, "Get up. Let's get back to fishing. We'll be available to talk and help later, but at this moment, the family needs to do whatever they need to do. Come on Billy, now."

"Maybe we should leave a day early. I feel like shit about what happened. Maybe they'd heal better if I wasn't around," Billy suggested.

"I don't know how you were involved, and I don't want to know," said Twin. "But whatever it was, you're not to blame. This is their family stuff and you got caught in it. Let's just finish out our trip."

"I sure wish I didn't have had to pollute the river with that gun," said Chief, following his two friends back up river.

&

"They all went back to their fishing," I said to Cynthia as I entered our campsite. I was afraid of what I might encounter. Not that I'm afraid of Loren—it is Cynthia who I fear. I have no idea of her perceptions or her feelings. How does one begin to process an event like this? Her future changed while she was quietly reading a book in her camp chair.

Cynthia looked up from her book, as if it were any other camping afternoon. Her eyes were red and swollen. "Just like males, not wanting to deal with stress, hoping that it will magically disappear."

Her statement was a relief—perhaps she's not angry with me, and maybe she'd be willing to talk about it. "Loren's car is gone," I said. "Did Loren leave?"

"Yes, he's driven off. I'm worried about him. He's so angry and I don't know how much he's been drinking. Stacey, tell me the truth. What happened out there? He said you seduced him, but that makes no sense at all."

"You're right, Cynthia. I did not seduce my brother, but what happened is not all his fault. I'm to blame for part of it and I need to be honest. I'd like your advice after you hear my side."

I recounted all yesterday's events, including the encounter with Billy in the Enterprise motel. I said I felt guilty, but admitted the allure of sex with a man not my husband. Then I just kept going and told Cynthia much more than I'd intended to disclose. I said I've been struggling with boredom and the slow retreat of my youth. And how, during this past week, with a few new males showing me positive attention, my passion amplified. I admitted I was attracted to Billy because he was so interested in me. I said I'd overreacted.

"Oh," said Cynthia with a pained expression. "I can't believe I'm so clueless to everything going on around me. Just when I think I knew people."

Cynthia has every right to think of me as the self-centered woman I obviously am. I have no intention of running from blame for my part in all this. I should never have let things get so out of control with Billy. But I will not diminish the behavior of my brother. That part is solely on him.

"I sent Billy a vibe that I wanted to spend time alone with him today. Nothing had been planned before we walked off together, but we wound up standing on the path along the river, kissing. That's when Loren came upon us. I don't know what would have happened if he hadn't interrupted us, and that's what worries me most about myself. I take risks that get my feelings rising to a point beyond my ability to reverse. I let my emotions direct my behavior, and only later do I feel ashamed. I must be crazy thinking that I'll be able to turn this off, or that I'll be able to get away with something without any scars. For God's sake, Cody was just down the trail."

"Did Loren break up the kiss before it got to be anything more?" Cynthia asked.

"Yes. Loren didn't see more than a kiss, because there *was* nothing more. But the kiss implied more than a vacation friendship. The kiss gave Loren the excuse to demean me, which has been an issue between us going back to our childhoods. The origin was anger and frustration with each other. Lord knows I flaunted my sexuality right in his face. Especially with his friends. Loren knew our father favored me, and Loren resented that. But Dad's fondling of me was perverted, which he disguised as jest. He'd grab and pat my ass, and refer to me as sexy just about every day. Loren watched me accept the sexually abusive behavior from our father, but I never let my brother near me. I used it to flaunt power over Loren, who I disliked. I knew from an early age that I could stop my father whenever I chose, and Dad relied on that. But I wasn't sure I could stop Loren."

"What a sick family," said Cynthia in an arrogant and judgmental tone.

I let her comment pass because she is correct. But I want her to understand our family's history and come to her own decisions. So I continued.

"My mother would just giggle when she saw what Dad was doing, and she'd only half-heartedly chastise him because he was the ruler of the family. Nothing was reported to anyone outside the family. Mom was fearful that he'd walk out of their marriage, so she would excuse Dad's behavior by stating, 'boys will be boys.' But that adage never applied to Loren. Loren scared me and, from puberty on, I was careful not to be left alone with him. The last thing I would ever do is seduce Loren."

Cynthia now knew more about our family history than anyone else did, including my husband. She remained silent, apparently digesting my words. After a short pause I continued.

"The first time Loren tried being a 'boy' with me, he found out I knew where his testicles were located and that I was not afraid to retaliate in a way that might do him irreparable damage. He also found out I was willing to wait until a time when he least expected it. In an immature way, I liked my father's caresses and knew that

I could shame him into stopping. But I detested the thought of being treated the same by my brother. I think it made everyone happier when I left home, except maybe my father. Looking back now, I might have felt competitive with my mother, because her weaknesses bothered me. Without fully realizing it then, I think I used my father's attention as a way to hurt her too. I probably hoped that she'd act to protect me and do something to get his attention focused on her. But you are right, Cynthia. I'm probably sicker than I think. "

"Obviously, that is not a story Loren has ever revealed to me," said Cynthia. "And I'll keep it just between us. But I still want to know what he did to you today and how Harry got involved."

"Once he saw what I was doing with Billy, he chased Billy off by pulling out his gun, and then I guess he wanted me to pay attention to him in the same way I was engaging with Billy. When I refused, he wanted to humiliate and dominate me so he ordered me to my knees, threatening to tell my family about Billy if I refused. He acted as if he wanted oral sex. I don't think it was a sexual thing for him, nor likely something he'd planned. He saw an opportunity and reverted to his teenage resentments, but he couldn't get an erection and that frustrated him. I mocked him, which further infuriated him. He was so focused on his anger that he didn't hear the others rush up behind him. The next thing

I remember was the force of Harry's body as he crashed into the two of us. Luckily, Loren had already set his gun down before Harry leapt on him."

Cynthia was listening attentively and shaking her head from side to side. Finally, she said, "I heard Harry's scream, but when I got there, it was all over. I'm numb and embarrassed and all I can think about now is Harry. Is he okay?"

"I'm worried about Harry, too, as well as you and Cody," I said. "The men over there are not my concern, but all of us have been affected. The boys seem to be handling things well. We stayed by the river and took time to share our feelings before I returned to you. Harry is feeling good about having come to what he believes was my rescue. Although I didn't think of myself as really being in danger, it appeared to Harry and Cody that I was. I'd like to think Loren would have come to his senses and stopped without intervention. I noticed that Cody seemed to appreciate Harry's aggressiveness. I plan to talk with Cody about what he witnessed, and I'll certainly thank Harry, but I'll not force him to talk. If he wants to talk about it, better he do that with you."

"I'm glad they're not here right now," stated Cynthia. "I need time to think about how I will handle all of this. I should probably not assume what Harry thinks or feels."

"It's a good idea not to make any long-term plans yet. You can stay with us in Idaho if you need time. In a couple of days, you can drive up with Harry and we'll take the boys to school. Then you can return with me to our home in Boise if you want. I don't know what I'll tell Coach about all this, so it would be nice to have you with me," I said.

"I'm not sure, Stacey. I'm just not sure of anything right now."

Sharing my long-suppressed secrets with Cynthia changed our relationship. I'd never confided the truth about my own participation before, which gave me a sense of freedom and a new bond with my sister-in-law.

Cynthia cannot repair the fractured relationship between Loren and me, nor can she trust me in the way she had before. I think she believes what I said about Loren, which opens up an evil and sinful side to her husband. Twenty years with Loren taught her that talking to him gets her nowhere. And Loren will likely never tell her the truth.

"I'm glad that you are taking the time to evaluate your own role, Stacey, but my religious faith means I see your action as evil and sinful as well as Loren's. Perhaps your behavior is more stupid than sinister, but at least you feel remorse."

Cynthia also said she appreciated my offer of a place for her to stay. If she takes me up on it, she'd have time and space for emotions to settle, and her mind to clear. Perhaps reach a decision.

# Thirty-Eight: Harry

AFTER THE FIGHT WITH DAD, Cody and I walked together back to the fishing poles we'd left on the riverbank. We didn't talk because, at least for myself, I didn't know what to say. Twin's debriefing helped, but my thoughts were all over the place.

I'm surprised I feel no shame or embarrassment for Dad. I am not like him. It was right for me to do what I did. What Dad did is wrong. I am the only one who could have intervened. The results would have been far worse had it been anyone else. This is a family matter that needs a family solution. Because of Dad, there are no winners, only losers, in my family. How will this affect Mom? I want to erase her shame and embarrassment, but have no idea how to start. Mom and Dad need time without me being present to do whatever they need for themselves. I shouldn't go back to the campsite yet. I'll support Mom's decisions whichever way they go. If I go back to the campsite, will Dad be angry with me?

Then there's Aunt Stacey. I love and admire her so much. Dad has always resented her. I've wondered why, and been curious, but never pried into the reason why. I suspect that Dad doesn't like her free spirit attitude. She just doesn't care about Dad's all-consuming sense of hell-fire punishment.

I can't justify Dad's behavior and it's so illogical that I'm having a hard time feeling compassion for him. Can I forgive behavior that makes no rational sense? I still love Dad, but he's not the kind of man I want to be. I don't want to be full of fear and I don't want to spend all my time being resentful. Is Dad mentally ill?

# Thirty-Nine: Cody

I'M REALLY GRATEFUL THAT HARRY acted so quickly because otherwise, I'd have had to be the one removing Uncle Loren from Mom. I was so angry that I might have seriously hurt Uncle Loren. Harry didn't hesitate at all. He just jumped in there and was brave, which is quite impressive. I hadn't realized it, but Harry is stronger than I thought, and not just physically. I'd trust him to have my back if things got rough at college. Maybe rooming with Harry won't be so bad after all. I could sure use a friend getting started at college.

But what about Mom? She's always said she and I have similar personalities. We're good at flirting and getting our way with whatever we want. Mom sure can charm others, especially men. Do I do the same with girls?

"Harry?" I said.

"Yes?"

"Did you get the feeling that there was something going on between my mom and Billy?"

"You mean, besides being friends?" said Harry. "I don't think they're anything more than that. They seem attracted to each, but not like anything funny going on."

"I wonder if she put herself in a dangerous situation and angered your dad."

"No," said Harry. "You don't know my dad. He gets upset at everything. He makes up things in his mind and tries to convince my mom and me that they're true. I used to believe him, but he's just paranoid. Your mom did nothing to be ashamed of and she's been nothing but a wonderful aunt to me. Dad hates it that anyone else has any influence on me, or my mom."

"My dad is so easy going that it drives me and Mom crazy," I said. "He seems to take us for granted, but is concerned about his students and the guys he coaches. I'm sure it's not easy on my mom. But don't get me wrong, he's not abusive or anything. In fact, Billy and his friends have talked to me more personally this past week than my dad has in a year. I should welcome the help of older guys when they take the time to give me what my dad doesn't."

"I just hope you never have to physically fight your father. I can't believe I just fought mine."

"You know, Harry, I can't see that ever happening. But who knows?" I said.

# Forty: Harry

I LEFT CODY WHERE HE'D BEEN FISHING and moved upstream in search of Chief.

If I've learned anything about the type of man to model myself after, this Native American fisherman who seems most at home in the wilderness comes closest. Chief doesn't need other people, especially the kind who carry baggage. And I'm impressed with the work he does relating to conservation and ecology. These last few days watching Chief has given me a direction to follow at the university.

"Mind if I watch you fish for a while?" I asked Chief when I found him. "I'd love to get down that cast of yours."

"Practice, Harry, practice," said Chief. "And remember to relax."

"Do you think I did the right thing back there with my dad? I just reacted; I didn't plan my moves at all. I've never stood up to my father before. I hope I didn't hurt him. He's probably already justified his behavior, or left for Boise all pissed-off."

"Just hurt his pride is all. He'll heal over."

"Chief, did you ever fight your dad?" I asked.

"No. He died before I was your age, but when he was alive, there were times I sure wanted to."

"I've never really understood my dad and right now I just feel disgusted, but I still love him. I'm glad I did what I did, but I feel bad for him and hope he doesn't hurt too much."

"Listen now 'cause this is the most important lesson you'll learn about fly fishing," said Chief while continuing to cast majestically. "When you catch a fish of any size, you must return him to his habitat with the least amount of stress and harm. It takes practice to do it well, but it is more important than the cast, the catch, or the fight."

"Your friend, Twin, showed me how to release. You crush the barb on the hook with needle-nosed pliers so you can remove the hook easier and with less strain on the fish."

"That's good," said Chief. "You also don't want to play the fish for too long, especially if the water is warm. A big fight, or a long fight is often done just for your satisfaction, but it's a selfish act and makes it harder for the fish to recover."

"But isn't the thrill of fishing rooted in the fight with the fish as he jumps and struggles to break free?" I asked.

"No. The thrill is to meet with the swimmers, connect with them for a short while, greet them with respect, and then let them return to what they were doing, a bit wiser. I try to do my best to make the length of the greeting as short as possible. Always have the proper equipment ready to remove the hook quickly. Look to see how he is hooked and back the hook out the same way it went in. Like removing a splinter from your finger, never rip the flesh. I also don't remove the fish from the water, if possible, and always touch him gently with wet hands on his belly, not near his gills. I point him upstream and place him in the most gentle current near me. I don't want him released in rushing water. He might need a little time to gather his strength. When he is ready, he will swim from my caress. Some will linger for a while and I have even had some return to my hand because, to my way of thinking, they appreciate the way I treat them."

"Chief, do you think they sense your native ways and feel a greater bond with you?" I asked.

"I wouldn't say that because in my culture we have always fished for food. Never released any of them, so I imagine, if anything, they would be more fearful if they saw me coming," laughed Chief. "We do have a different mindset about the food we eat than folks who have always bought food from a store. However, when I keep a fish to eat, I bless him and thank him for the honor of his sacrifice just as I will someday receive the blessing of the world that I leave behind. At that time, I will become food for the plants and animals that remain after me."

"Do you ever take a trophy fish?"

"Never have, but that's just me. I also don't take pictures of my best catches, unless, of course, the fish asks for a photo," said Chief, this time really laughing.

"So the important thing seems to be the release—more important than the catch," I said.

"Exactly. The interaction of the catch is exciting, but the skill needed for release is what makes the whole cycle complete. Always remember that. And the word 'fisherman' starts with the letters f-i-s-h, remember that. Now go and gently release your dad."

I watched as Chief modeled what he had just preached. Chief was relaxed as he handled the fish and he took care to keep it from being traumatized. I need to practice that skill. I need to do my best to allow the wound from the hook to heal as easily as possible.

&

I connected with Cody before heading back to camp. I was tired and hungry, and looking forward to dinner and sleep. I think we both were.

"Your father has gone back home," Mom said. "And I need to talk to you about that."

So I followed Mom out of camp and back to the river. She seems to have a new attitude of determination and decisiveness. I wonder if she's disappointed in me for attacking Dad. Does she think I've abandoned him? If she's disappointed in me, that would be my biggest regret. She wasn't there to see me do it, and doesn't know why I did. I don't really want to talk to her about all this. No matter what I say, one of my parents will be hurt.

But I can't imagine living the rest of my life with a secret. Maybe this was the best way to untie my connection to my parents and make my own way in life. I've been looking forward to moving to Moscow, but only because Mom and Dad provided me with a safety net.

Mom and I sat down by the river, both of us leaning against a tree.

"Harry, I'm proud of you for defending Aunt Stacey. I don't know all the details and don't think I want to, but I know enough. Your father has problems he wrestles with, and those problems came out today in a way that required someone to stop him. Someday I'm sure he'll agree that he lost control and that it was good you interceded and prevented him from any further devastating behavior. You actually saved him too, and I thank you for that. But I want to hear how you feel about what took place."

"Mom, I wish he had never come here," I said. "The minute he showed up, everything changed and got heavy. I don't dislike him or anything. In fact, I still love him, but I'm glad I kicked his ass."

"It probably should have been me, long ago, who did that, not you. I've had to put up with his domineering crap and sarcasm for too long. By allowing him to act like that, I'm just as responsible for this as he is."

"Don't think that way, Mom," I said. "This must have been brewing a long time. It's not our fault and I hope it's over. I hate his superior attitude and I don't ever want to fight him again."

"So, how about this? We'll go home tomorrow and spend a couple of days getting your stuff packed for college. Your father will likely give us plenty of space and he'll be happy to hear I don't need his help to drive you to Moscow. That way, he won't miss work and won't have to deal with facing what happened today. He'll just harbor himself until the storm subsides."

"But Mom, I hate to run off to school and leave you alone to deal with Dad if he's still angry. I'll worry about you."

"Let's see how your dad acts. Aunt Stacey offered me a place to stay with them for a while. To give me a time for thinking and pondering. I may take her up on that."

"I'd feel better if you did. You know, Mom, I'm so

glad you're not mad at me. I will support whatever decision you make. I can live without Dad's support if that's the way he wants it, but I need you and your love for me."

Mom stood up and wrapped her arms around me. I'm so glad she'll be in my future. I sure want to be in hers.

# Forty-One: Stacey

"CODY, I NEED TO KNOW THAT WE WILL RETURN to McCall okay with each other."

"What do you mean, Mom?" I said. "Of course we're all right. Uncle Loren flipped out and you were the victim. I'm glad Harry stepped up and took care of business. Otherwise, I would have, and it wouldn't have been pretty."

"Well, I've learned a big lesson. I won't be developing friendships with men if it could embarrass those I love," I said. "I don't care about your Uncle Loren, but I certainly don't want to jeopardize the relationships of the people I really care about like you, your Aunt Cynthia, and Harry."

"You can be kind of flirty around new people, Mom, but that doesn't bother me and I don't think it bothers Dad, but that's because we know you're just playing around. You don't mean anything by it."

Cody's statement was revealing, but it also hurt. Although, fortunately, it implied Cody wasn't aware of how far I'd gone with Billy, it also signified that his impression of me was not entirely true. Flirtatious and vain, yes. Trustworthy, no. It's bad enough to think Cody views me as a shallow, attention-seeking person who uses her looks to attract friends, but he thinks I can control myself. I had better change my ways and make every effort to live up to his expectations. It also hurts to think he might have learned bad behavior from me—like using his physical gifts to get what he wants.

"You're right about why I do that sort of thing, Cody," I said. "And you're right about my desire not to hurt anyone, but I've got to stop all that flirting before it gets me in trouble. If you catch me being overly nice to men, especially those who are easily played, bring it to my attention. Just say something like, 'Mom, your plastic surgeon is on the phone about an overdue bill."

"Or, maybe I should say that Dad is recovering nicely from the three-goon beating you ordered."

Hearing Cody's humor was such a relief to me. The collusion of my oldest son in my quest to change my behavior might work just fine. We now share a secret that bonds us, and perhaps will help rein in a destructive personality trait we share.

"And if I see you manipulating some young, innocent female," I said, "I'll stop you in your tracks by saying, 'Cody, have you renewed the stalking order on that pretty policewoman you met in your last anger management class?'"

&

Our last camp dinner was fresh trout fillets that Chief gave to Harry to share with us. It was a nice gesture by an older man showing approval of Harry for the keen interest he demonstrated this week. That, and approval for the decisive action Harry demonstrated when his father was in the wrong.

In some cultures, teenage boys go on quests to signify and solidify their passage into manhood. That doesn't happen in our culture, but sometimes teens are ready when a quest appears. Chief seems to appreciate the full importance of this growth milestone for Harry and his gift of fish implies he is aware Harry's defining moment came today.

I'm happy to be having a family meal tonight, without including the camping men. I feel accepted just as I am by my son and sister-in-law. My secrets are out there, totally exposed, but I feel closer to them than ever before.

Cynthia seems happy her son is poised to succeed at school and in life. With my help, she'll deal with Loren in a far different way than the family's old patterns. She's demonstrated a determination to move forward—with Loren, or not.

Cody and Harry are more attentive tonight. All four of us pitched in with dinner and clean up. After the meal, we sat around the fire and told stories, none of which touched on today's events. This is our last dinner together, and that makes me sad.

Cody seems more relaxed with Harry tonight and allowed his cousin to lead the conversation whenever Harry had something to say. It is apparent to me that Cody is enjoying Harry's company. I see the pleasure in my son's eyes. He looks stronger, and more relaxed than he's been all week.

I've been communicating my gratitude to Harry all evening by being attentive to him when he speaks and by sending him smiling glances. Nothing flirtatious, of course. Just an indication that I was proud of him. I could actually feel the difference. One intention comes from the head; the other comes from somewhere deeper. I believe Harry received my messages of gratitude and perhaps feels even closer to me now. He has an aunt who genuinely loves and appreciates him.

Cynthia must have grave concerns about her own future—with or without her husband. But her son is his own man now. And the boys have bonded. Cody has become a true friend to Harry. I couldn't have asked for more for both our kids.

# Forty-Two: Chief

MY THOUGHTS ARE FOCUSED ON THE THRILL of the moment. I am waist-deep in water, but firmly planted on the stones that define this river's bottom. I thank the protective spirit that allows me to stand here on this firm ground that so many before me have travelled.

The current of the river is home to the fish and water plants that feed off nutrients and oxygen. This flow, this movement of nutrition, is the essence of life in its most basic sense. The lower half of my body appreciates that flow of liquid vital to all life. I am also made of the same liquid and, in time, will flow past to sustain what I leave behind.

My upper body is surrounded by the fresh air so necessary for my existence. Sometimes, I do not give thought to its importance, but if I lose my footing—as sometimes happens—and get caught in the flow of the swimmers' environment, I marshal my efforts to return to air. I am not yet ready to enter the sustaining flow of life.

I am right where I long to be. The flight of the artificial fly as it swirls and dances through the air, the result of unconscious movement and rhythm orchestrated by my upper body, helps me sort out the events of this past week.

Billy and Twin will soon begin their trip back toward the Oregon coast and resume their lives. At times, they lose their footing but they are survivors of war and two decades of adult life. Those experiences provide them with confidence and the wisdom to proceed with whatever comes next.

Billy will think of Stacey, of that I have no doubt. Perhaps he will fantasize a life with her, but not to the point that it weakens his marriage or causes him to chance future contact. This week might even rejuvenate and enhance the love he shares with his wife. Perhaps next year, Billy will hope Stacey shows up again. But the purpose of their friendship was concluded this week.

Twin enjoyed the two teenagers. His brother, his mirrored self, is long gone. Now he lives a life surrounded by females, appropriately so, because who better can know the male hidden from him. A wife and two daughters sustain him in the best of health, yet are unable to provide the male camaraderie that Twin experienced this week. He was teacher, mentor, and friend to the cousins on the cusp of adulthood. The interaction was as good for him as it was for them.

I hear an engine start. I hear the tires of Twin's truck turn onto the gravel road that will lead my friends out of the Eagle Cap Wilderness. They have a longer trip than I do, so they always leave sooner, allowing me a few more precious hours to fish alone. I'm already packed, but I'm not ready to leave. I must take this one last walk in the river.

The two Idaho boys, on the threshold of manhood, are ready for a new adventure. Perhaps Cody realizes he will no longer be the oldest and most beloved child as he enters the river of young adults in college. None of them will be interested in catering to him.

Cody and Harry, as a team, will be able to safely negotiate that new territory. This week, Cody learned he can count on Harry, and that Harry's influence will help draw him into the mainstream of student life. Cody's inclination will be to socialize with the favored few, but Harry will provide entrance into alternative lifestyles. He is learning that charm isn't the only path to success. His future will be shaped by his intellectual pursuits, not only athletics. To my way of thinking, Cody is far more ready for his future than he was a week ago.

I suspect Stacey and Billy shared more this week than a goodbye kiss. Stacey seems to have learned she is capable of redirecting the flow of life, not just creating a few ripples. Her charisma projects her engaging personality in ways that feed into the fantasies of both sexes. She communicates whatever message the others want to hear, but maybe she now realizes that her gift can be a curse. Perhaps she needs no further wake-up call. The woman flirted with fate this week. Perhaps she'll be more careful and less playful with the emotions of others from now on.

I identify most with Cynthia, the quiet mother concerned with everyone except herself. But life is rife with bittersweet experiences. I suspect her marriage is in crisis and there's no easy decision ahead. Her strong religious faith and the support from the women in her church will help. Cynthia is smart enough to sort the wheat from the chafe. It's time for Cynthia to release Harry into the wild, and she will do it with love and kindness.

Harry doesn't need to analyze his own behavior. The boy is intuitive. He found comfort in the natural environment and I believe he will carry that with him no matter where he goes.

I watched Harry become a fly fisherman this week—it's not hard to tell when it gets into someone's blood. And it's not hard to imagine that I'll meet Harry on some isolated stretch of river somewhere. I have no doubt the boy will pass it on to those who come behind him.

Swirling around me are the majestic trout that have lived here since the beginning, sharing the water with plant life and insects that understand the balance of life in this pristine setting. The fish understand the Great Spirit's wilderness that is, for the moment, shared with a man and a gun, one of which is settling peacefully on the river's bottom.

&

By the time I left the river and drove away, all evidence of human inhabitance had been erased from our campsites. The pine needles, the roaring river, the craggy peaks of the mountains, and all the rest that comprise this isolated wilderness are back to what existed long before human interruption. The wilderness has been released to return to what it has always been.

# About the Author

GUS WILLEMIN began the first 17 years of his trip in New York City. There have been many stops along the way—some short, some lengthy, including San Diego and currently Newport, Oregon. Throughout the journey, he has compiled many titles—some short-lived, some not. Son, brother, husband, father, friend, Marine, student, teacher, counselor, musician, fisherman, inmate, classmate, in-law, and outlaw. He's dabbled in it all and mastered nothing. He has no regrets, and plans to stay put until asked to leave.